The
JADE
SUN

Realm of the Prophets
Book II

E J Doble

Cover design and illustration by: Liam Fraser @lafgraphic

For Liam,

For your artistry, your craft,
and your kindness.

The sun rose and fell. The moon and the stars passed overhead. Dunes stretched on for impossible miles.

And the people of Arbash had left their home.

It had been their home for millennia, given to them by ancient wanderers, or so the story went: the Prophets had come from the desert long ago; they had placed the first stones of what would become their great city; they had drawn wells of water from the earth, bringing life and splendour to the land. They had nurtured it, and prospered from it, and life had been good.

And when, after some time, the Prophets inevitably passed on – ascending from the world to reach the stars above – the inheritors of Arbash had appeared from the desert and claimed the great city as their own. They had walked its empty streets, and peered into its empty windows, and they had believed that the vast and beautiful land must have been destined for them all along. They did not know how it had come to be, nor who had built such an impressive place – but something about the citrus bushes and the shimmering blue sea had seemed to call to them, as if it were where they belonged. A place that would sustain them forever.

A place to call home, at last.

So the city grew, and the people with it, and the once-empty streets of Arbash bustled with life. Culture sprang forth like blossom on a young tree; decadence and abundance and splendour abounded. Decades passed, rolling into centuries, until the inheritors believed the city had always been theirs, and that they had been there since the dawn of the World itself at the earliest point in time. It was by their hand that Arbash had been built, and it was by their hand that it continued to prosper – and the Prophets, long forgotten in their absence, were cast as little more than a memory, their stories long eroded.

From thereon, the Prophets were seen only in what they had left behind, bubbling up from the earth in tiny springs and budding from the groves of beautiful clementines. Their faces still adorned some of the city's outer walls, and their teachings were woven on the faded tapestries within the God-Elect's elegant palace. They were the subject of myths and legends, sung about in communal halls and whispered quietly in bedtime stories. And even though those stories lacked some of the truth in their retellings, the message beneath it all had always remained the same about the Prophets: that life would go on, and they would persevere no matter the odds.

And even on the darkest of nights, it was hope that always shined brightest.

The sun rose and fell. The moon and stars passed overhead. The people of Arbash continued to prosper.

Until something appeared from the sea.

It had been a dot, at first, on the distant horizon, coming and going like a comet. It had hardly been noticed by the people of Arbash at first; it had hardly been worth mentioning to those in charge. So they had let it pass by with barely a whisper, and no cause of fuss or alarm.

How wrong they turned out to be.

Sometime later, an enemy appeared at the cove, bringing swords and fire with them for all to see and fear. They had come on the backs of boats, and set up camps, and marched up the hillside toward the city's huge gates. They had come with purpose, and a desire in their eyes.

And a single goal, with a swift and certain end.

The people of Arbash – having never seen such a perilous sight – had been lost and had not known what to do. Their home was the only one they had ever known, one they had built with their own hands. To abandon it, and flee into the desert, was to abandon everything they held closest to them. Life would never be the same again, and they were running out of time.

And yet, even with the fear stirring in their hearts, one young girl had stood out amongst them, and convinced the people of Arbash that the desert was the only way. Backed by the wisdom of the God-Elect, with the Prophets watching on from the stars high above, she had told them that home was not within their walls, but was instead within their hearts. That with hope and faith, to avoid the shackles of their enemy, fleeing into the desert was all they had left. Their ancestors had come from the desert long ago in search of a new life, after all.

And it was there that the people of Arbash would have to return, in the hope they would live long enough to see a new life of their own.

The sun continued to rise and fall. The moon and stars passed overhead.

And out in the desert many miles from the city of Arbash, a new kind of destiny was being born.

The Prophets had come from the desert long ago, in search of a place to call home. They had travelled far and wide, and had suffered many failures along the way. By luck or by chance, they had happened upon the valley leading to the beautiful blue sea, and had built there a wonderful sanctuary that would last for millennia to come. They had built it up from the ground, and left it to their successors, and had watched on from the stars ever since.

And now, from those same stars, the Prophets looked down on the people of Arbash, and the new Prophet who had come to lead them. The young girl with the world in her heart, imparting hope on those around her. Traversing the dunes, stretching endlessly beyond, searching for signs of life and sanctuary as the old Prophets once had.

For history is cyclical, and those who come after walk the same paths as those before. Footprints mark the sands and fade away moments later, but the memory of the step will always remain.

The Prophets had come from the desert long ago, and had found a place to last millennia.

Now a new Prophet had stepped out from their shadow.

Looking for the next place to call home.

I

THE DESERT

I

Stood on the crest of a great dune, looking out on the desert beyond, My'ala inhaled the cool night air and gazed up at the twinkling stars. There were thousands of them up there: tiny dots of light, as numerous as the grains of sand beneath her feet. Some formed in clusters, while others stood alone, shining brightly with dashes of colour. Many of the larger ones looked almost like eyes, their pupils alive with activity.

My'ala wondered for a moment if any of them were watching her, just then. If these vast, beautiful, distant things, sleeping in the day and emerging at night, were looking down on the great sands of the Unknown, following their path across the desert. Perhaps they were waiting for something. Perhaps they were longing for a sign. Or perhaps they were there to simply watch the days go by, shining brightly with all the time in the world.

Stood at the crest of the dune, My'ala looked upon them in wonder and smiled. It had been over seven suns since they had left the walls of Arbash, but her amazement at the night sky had not dimmed by any measure. It watched over them every night, and they awaited its return every day. It brought a coolness to the air, and quelled some of the soreness in their feet. It was a blessing, in many ways, if she dared call it that.

A sign of hope, she thought, *that one day this may yet be our home.*

She drew herself up to full height and let a long breath go, thinking on that hope as it spread out for many long miles in all directions. Over every rolling dune, and in every fragile oasis, stretching far and wide until My'ala felt so very small all of a sudden, under the vastness of the Beyond, in the middle of the Unknown. A tiny speck in an impossible world, with only the wind and the stars to keep her company.

Wondering which way to go...

"A beautiful night, My'ala, is it not?"

The voice made her jump suddenly — thinking she had been alone on the dune — and made her heart miss a beat in her chest. Turning her head, she saw the silver-blonde hair and shimmering blue eyes of the God-Elect at her shoulder, wearing long white robes with strips of crimson red and delicate gold woven in along the seams. His approach up the sandbank to her right had been completely silent, and part of her almost believed he had just manifested from thin air.

Makes me think I need to be on my guard more, My'ala mused with a smile. *Not that his company is a problem, that is.*

Since their departure from Arbash, the city's young leader

had spent increasing lengths of time with My'ala and her family, acknowledging her new figurehead position among the citizens of the city. It had been her rallying speech, after all, that had convinced them to head out into the desert in the first place – a fact that My'ala was reminded of regularly, and held in the pit of her stomach like an angry snake.

"It is beautiful, yes," she replied, holding her abdomen.

"I've always found the stars rather remarkable," the God-Elect expressed with a glint in his eye. "So far away and yet so very close to us."

"Watching over us, almost."

"I've always noticed how they reflect so clearly in people's eyes, too, when they look up at them." He smiled. "It's almost like we're trying to decipher the secrets of the Beyond, looking up into the dark as we do…"

My'ala acknowledged him with a nod of her head, feigning any interest, but her thoughts were suddenly elsewhere. She detached from the conversation – from the world, even – as a collection of thoughts bubbled in her mind. Memories, like a blooming flower, unravelling petal after petal, until one image filled her mind unequivocally, accompanied by a single name.

Artemis, she thought, taking a long draw of breath.

Gods, Artemis…

It was the first time she had thought of him since their departure from the city, with the stress of keeping everyone together overriding any other thought. Her duties and new-found responsibility had left everything that had happened over the previous few weeks as a blur, never quite affixing one place in her head. It was only when she stopped and thought on it as she did then, that she realised just how much had actually happened in that time, and how close she had been to forgetting.

She was overcome with a sense of guilt, looking out over the purple dunes ahead with an eerie blue horizon all around. That someone so important to her – someone that had guided her through so much, and had given her so much advice – had slipped from her mind so easily. His words had been her solace since she was a child; his teachings, had been what had saved the people of Arbash and convinced them to flee. In the end, he had been integral to everything, without her even realising it.

And yet I nearly forgot about him, My'ala thought, with a knot in her heart pulling slowly tighter. *What kind of person does that make me? He was the one person who stood by me the most when things got tough… the one person who got me through it all.*

Looking up again to the stars, she imagined his face there among the constellations, forming in the spaces in-between. His long beard and his flowing robes, and the deep wells of his eyes. The pipe held between his lips, with the silver round of a crescent moon laced between his fingers. So old and so wise, and so remarkable all in one.

I'm sorry, Artemis… I'm so sorry that I nearly forgot you, she considered, holding a hand to her chest. As she did so, she could almost make out the lines of the stars forming into a smile. *I'll show you my appreciation one day, old friend.*

I promise you that.

"My'ala?"

She turned slowly to the God-Elect, returning to reality in a daze, to find him studying her with a deep concern behind his eyes. All she could offer in response was a blink.

"Is everything okay?" he asked.

"I…" She gulped, forcing a smile – hiding the glassy sheen

over her pupils. "Yes, I…" She sighed. "It's… it's just been a long few days out here in the desert, is all."

"Of course." He gave an effortless smile, and bowed his head in understanding. "We have travelled very far, and undergone much change. These things… can do their damage to us over time. The feelings you have, and no doubt the weight you feel on your shoulders, is shared by every one of us here, I imagine."

"It's just that, this is like nothing we've ever known before… not since the old, *old* times when the first nomads came to Arbash and founded the city long ago." The mention of her homeland angered the snake in her stomach, which coiled over itself in its fury.

"Our ancestors, yes."

"We're out on our own, here… against the odds… praying that there's somewhere we can go. Somewhere we can stay, and *survive,* even. And… I guess I just hope there *is,* one day. That there is some place to call home… at the end of all this."

Sensing her unease, the God-Elect took a single step forward – gesturing for the two guards lingering at his back to stand down – and placed a hand on her shoulder, the blue light of his eyes almost like shards of lightning.

"You know, My'ala… when you spoke that day, on the platform next to me back in Arbash… you did something very special, and very important. Not something any of us expected from you, it's true, but you were perhaps the only person who could have said it in a way that we all understood." He touched his chest, over his sternum as if gesturing to his soul. "You gave the people of Arbash *hope*… you gave them hope when they didn't have any, and thought they never would again. You showed them a path forward – you showed *me* a path forward, too – that we would have never believed was open to us, had it not been for you. You gave us a chance… and you saved us from what would've happened if we had stayed."

"I was just doing what I felt was right…"

"And you succeeded, in so many ways by doing so. You showed us the way forward… and you give so much hope to every citizen who follows us even now, out in the Unknown that surrounds us. You are a beacon to them, in so many ways: a guiding light to bring them out of the darkness."

He leaned in close to her, and gestured over the dune to where the glints of torchlight could be seen.

"They believe in you, My'ala, every single one of them… and I think it's past time that you started believing in yourself, too, if we're to get through this all together."

The God-Elect squeezed her shoulder gently and took a step back, sliding his hand back beneath the folds of his robes.

Opposite him, My'ala stood for a moment and let his words roll over in her head, subduing the knot in the pit of her stomach that had formed over the previous days. Looking back on the day the last few weeks in Arbash, she remembered the wisdom that had been imparted on her by her mentor, and the wisdom she had then imparted on her fellow citizens in turn. She recalled the glow in their eyes from the podium as their burden was lifted, and they could finally step away from their fear of the end. Their comradery, and community, and relief. And she was reminded of their smiles, most of all, as bright as the pearly blue sea.

They believe there is somewhere out here for us, despite the struggles they know that they'll face, she thought, looking at the stars again. *They believe in that idea — in that vision of our future — and they believe I am the one to deliver it. Ever since that day on the podium… they look to me for their answers. They believe in me, against all odds.*

She breathed, and smiled, and closed her eyes.

And perhaps now I should too.

"Thank you, your Highness," she said, as the God-Elect returned to his guards.

"What for?" he asked, turning back to her briefly.

"You just… always seem to say exactly what I need to hear."

"I say the truth, My'ala… it needs to be said."

She bowed her head, and he did so in turn. "Thank you, your Highness."

"You're most welcome." He paused. "And please dispense with the *'your Highness'*, if you will… call me Aurelius instead. It'll be good to hear my true name again."

She smiled broadly, grateful for the knowledge he had imparted, and nodded.

"And just so that you're aware, the citizens have been ordered to set camp for the night and rest well for our journey in the morning, so there's no need to rush for the remainder of the evening," Aurelius added, brushing down his robes. "May I suggest you be close to your family tonight, and spend some quality time with them if you can. I imagine they will be needing you at the moment as much as you need them."

"Yes, of course, I… I shall… and thank you, again."

"My pleasure. Sleep well, My'ala."

"And you, Aurelius."

Turning from her once more, the God-Elect paced slowly down the dune toward the first scattering of tents, his two loyal guards following in tow with their helmets shining under the moon.

My'ala watched him walk away, disappearing slowly over the lip of the dune, until he slipped from sight like the desert winds and was gone as swiftly as he had appeared.

He's a single comet, passing through the endless Beyond, she thought, breathing deeply. A cold wind rippled up the sandbanks at her back and billowed against her robes. *And here I stand again, alone in the dark…*

Save for the thousands of stars, watching from high above.

II

Her family's tent sat at the west-most end of the camp, pointing almost like an arrowhead in the direction of the place they had once called home. Under a purple haze, it stood slightly adjacent to the other canopies, resting against a steep-sided dune where any noise was wiped away by the wind. It appeared solemn in the low light; one could even call it lonely. The clear separation of their tent from the others had no doubt been her father's decision, but whether that decision was made through a lack of trust, or to account for his easily-disturbed sleep, My'ala could not entirely tell.

In front of the main tent – beneath an overhang propped up on two poles – a small fire was burning delicately, its yellow-orange glow shining across the sand around it. Using salvaged wood from the desert, and a striking stone they had found in the evacuation, her family had been able to light a fire each night and keep themselves warm, while cooking whatever insects they found scurrying over the sand around them. The beetles and spiders were hardly the most appealing things to eat, and barely counted as a meal at the best of times, but out in the desert where every day was an uncertainty, even the smallest ant could be counted as a blessing.

Approaching the tent from the east, My'ala slowed her pace and took in the scene, looking out on the horizon opposite. She knew that, somewhere out in the vastness beyond, the tall spires and round domes of Arbash could be seen out towards the sea, where they had been for longer than time and would remain longer still. Nestled in the bowl of a valley, with rows of bushes spilling down to a pearly blue sea, and a single ancient tree sat on a hillside just to the south. It had been a tranquil place: one that she could conjure an image of in an instant, and held on to as if holding a breath she never wished to let go.

But reality was different than that. It was harsher, in many ways. As My'ala looked out on the sands that they had just crossed, tracing all the way back to the gates of their home, she realised that their footprints and tracks had already been lost to the desert. The ruts of their cart wheels and the drag lines of their tent poles had completely disappeared. There was no sign that they had ever been there, or that they had travelled all that way at all. Their past had gone with the winds, and their present was all that remained: camped out in a dip in the dunes under the watchful gaze of the stars, holding on to the one thing that the desert could not sweep away.

Ourselves.

She took a deep breath and carried on ahead, pulling her gaze away from the horizon as she approached her family's tent. Even from afar, the glow of the fire danced across her boots and through the furrows of her robes.

Aurelius told me to take some time with my family because they need me as much as I need them, My'ala recalled.

And with this longing in my chest, I think I'm starting to understand what he meant by that.

"Mi-Mi!" came a call from beside the fire. A shadow rose to

meet her, rushing out from under the overhang to wrap My'ala in their arms.

The scent of honeysuckle caught in My'ala's nose almost immediately, and a warmth blossomed in her heart that threatened tears in her eyes.

"Hello, ma," she replied, pressing her hands against her mother's back.

"It's good to see you, Mi-Mi… it's so good to see you."

"You don't mind if I come and sit with you at the fire, do you…?"

"No, of course, of course! There's no need to ask, ever." She stepped back suddenly and held My'ala's shoulders, smiling softly. Her deep leathery skin appeared so delicate in the low light, betraying her age, with the tiny furrows of wrinkles over her cheeks hardly noticeable. There was a youthful illumination behind her irises like tiny candles, full of love and wonder. Stood as they were then, with only the light of the moon to see, My'ala realised just how much her mother looked like Su'la in that moment.

And I suppose like me too, now I think of it.

"There isn't much food to go around I'm afraid," her mother commented, guiding her towards their fire. "We've salvaged what we can from the supplies, and your da has managed to find a few insects to roast. I know it's not the most pleasant food, but please do have some…"

"I will ma, don't worry, I will."

My'ala stepped under the canopy and took in the fire's delicate warmth, letting it soothe her aching muscles. The sudden heat radiated across her skin, drawing colour back into her pimpled cheeks and revitalising her numb fingers. It reminded her of the cooking pots they used to use back home, with the smoke filtering up through a funnel at the apex of their roof. The thought immediately made her stomach growl, teasing her with hunger.

Although she didn't pay the sensation that much attention, as she peered over the lingering flames and spied the moon-like round of a person's face sat opposite her – a person who she gravitated to almost instantly, opening her arms out wide to wrap them in a welcoming hug.

"Hello, Mi," her father chirped, sliding his arm over her shoulders and giving her a pat. He smelt of metal and sweat. "It's good to see you."

"And you, da... always."

"Please, have a seat with us. I can't say there's much going in terms of food, but you're welcome to... whatever you can stomach."

Taking the offer, My'ala lowered onto a flat stone between her parents and adjusted her robes, looking over to her father as she did so. He sat watching the fire, lost in his own world for a moment, and the deep lines through his face reminded her of the bark of a tree.

He doesn't look well, My'ala acknowledged, rolling her finger and thumb together. The sudden change and evacuation of Arbash had taken its toll on him, she knew: he was more watchful and cautious, and had a darkness about his eyes that put him way beyond his years. Every movement he made or step he took had an uncertainty to it, like he wasn't sure of what was right and wrong. Every tiny gesture and nod of the head had so much buried beneath it, which was always left unsaid.

Even then, sat there tending to the fire, she spied a slight tremble in his wrists as his eyes flitted from the fire to the wider camp, and his hand lingered at his side as if to pick up an imaginary sword. My'ala could make little sense of it, having seen him repeat the same action for several nights' past. He appeared to be constantly on-edge, unsettled by something, clenching his toes in the sand to match the rapid beats of his heart. But out on the rolling dunes of the great Unknown, with nothing threatening around them for dozens of leagues, My'ala could never quite ascertain what kind of thing he really feared.

Who knows, she thought, pulling her hair behind her ear. *Maybe I should ask him——*

"Here you go, Mi-Mi," her mother said suddenly, pulling My'ala from her thoughts as a brass plate was dropped in her lap. The husky, charred remains of three dune beetles lay curled up on its surface, which My'ala would have been repulsed by had her stomach not growled so loudly.

"It's the best we can do… uh, sorry," her mother muttered, looking between her and the plate on her lap. "Sorry."

"It's… absolutely fine, thank you," she replied, lifting one beetle with her fingers and placing it on her tongue. The crunch it made as her teeth ground through it was enough to make her nauseous, but after several days of stomaching them a lot of the initial repulsion had gone.

"A bit of sea salt would make the beetles taste better, I reckon," her father said, using a charred stick to stoke the fire. "Almost like the stewed snakes we used to have. Damn, I miss those things…"

"Your da and I have been discussing what comforts we miss the most from home," her mother added. "He misses a lot of fineries like sea salt and spices and plump cushions, whereas I… well, I'm sure you can guess what I miss most."

My'ala thought for a moment, recalling her childhood in

Arbash as if it were a scar on her mind. "The hummingbirds?" she replied eventually.

Her mother smiled – a slightly pained expression, almost like sadness – and placed a hand against her knee. "No, my dear – although, I do of *course* miss those beautiful little birds." Her shoulders loosened. "No, the thing I miss the most is the gojan fruits! With their thick skins and fleshy insides…"

"…and the swirling patterns in the middle," My'ala recalled, nodding to herself. "Of course, yes, how… poor of me to forget…"

"No, no, it's no problem Mi-Mi! We all forget sometimes!" Her mother leaned in closer and rubbed her finger against My'ala's knee, a glassy sheen over her eyes like the scales of a fish. There was a trembling on her bottom lip that she tried desperately to hide.

Something's… not right, My'ala thought almost immediately, looking deep into her mother's pupils with an assessing stare. *You aren't telling me something. Or there's something you don't want me knowing. Because this – all of this – isn't normal.*

Not one bit.

She lowered her plate onto the floor and met her mother's gaze, rolling her tongue over her teeth. "Ma, is—"

A gasp caught in her left ear suddenly, stopping her train of thought.

She turned immediately, and caught sight of her father as he pressed a hand against his chest and coughed violently. He tried to breathe between the splutters, struggling to stay upright as the fit took hold and his face reddened—

My'ala panicked, pressing up on the balls of her feet like a cat, ready to leap forward and come to his aid – but no sooner had it started, than her father inhaled sharply and dispelled the coughing altogether, leaning against his thighs with veins straining in his neck.

"Da, are... are you okay?" My'ala murmured, shaken by the weakness of his breathing. "Da?"

"I'm..." Her father wheezed, exhaling slowly. "I'm alright, it's... it's just the air, the desert... all the sand...." He coughed a couple more times, gripping his chest until he finally sat upright and purged the pain from his system. "I'm... fine..."

"Why are you coughing so much? Do you need anything? A cloth mask or something?"

"We've already tried, Mi-Mi," her mother replied in his stead. "This coughing he gets is quite severe, and once it starts it can't really be stopped. It usually happens more in the evenings – probably after travelling for so long – and sleep appears to be the best cure."

"Well, if he gets too tired from walking, then I... I can order the cart-handlers to free space on their caravan for you, if you need it..."

"And take the seats of those who are *actually* infirm, who then have to *suffer* the journey with the rest of us? Absolutely not." His emphasis on the word '*suffer*' caught in My'ala's head, and the snake in the pit of her stomach rattled its tail. "I may be struggling with this blasted cough... but I am not about to make anyone else's life harder when I still have two legs and can walk like the rest. I'll get used to it eventually... at some point..."

Staring at him – through him, in many ways – My'ala found herself without words, and lowered her gaze from him in silence. She knew he had been struggling with the change, and the new way of life that the people of Arbash had adopted – but to see his health take a toll as it had, was enough to make her want to weep there and then.

This isn't fair…

Sensing My'ala's distress, her mother squeezed her knee and lifted from her seat, peering across the fire at the dejected man opposite. "I think it's about time we got some rest… wouldn't you say so too, my dear?"

Looking up, her father remained blank-faced for a moment, before nodding and rising to his own shaky stand. "I would tend to agree, yes… it'd probably do me some good."

"Excellent." My'ala watched her mother turn to her. "Mi-Mi, could you do me a favour, my sweet?"

"Of course, ma," she replied, unsure of what else to do.

"Your sister went off over the ridge to the west a while ago, saying she wanted some time to think… would you be able to go and check on her for me, and maybe try and coax her back? We have a long day tomorrow, I imagine… and I, well…" Her voice tapered off. "Just… see if she'll get some rest soon for me, please."

My'ala managed a smile in reply, the nerves bristling up her spine as she stood and brushed herself off. "I'll go and find her and bring her back here, ma, no problem."

"Thank you, Mi."

Her mother leaned in and kissed her forehead, before turning to her father and gesturing towards the tent's entrance. Watching him turn away, she saw how the lines across his face had deepened immeasurably, almost like tilled soil.

"Be safe, My'ala," her father exclaimed, almost as a whisper.

"And you…" she replied in turn, as he drifted toward the folds of the tent and disappeared inside.

Leaving My'ala with a tear trailing down her cheek, wondering what was going on.

III

To the far west of the camp, over two dunes that had formed like sidewinding serpents, My'ala found her sister sat with her back to the camp, looking out over the sands in the rough direction of home. The horizon beyond was slowly shifting, passing from blue to black as twilight crept in, and the stars above expanded across the sky in dazzling clusters of light. Night was nearly upon them, clutching at the corners of the Unknown, drawing them to slumber in preparation for the coming dawn.

A reality they all knew – perhaps the only one left to them now.

Approaching her sister with quiet, padding steps, My'ala sat down next to Su'la in silence and gazed out at the sandy peaks beyond, taking in the night air. They remained that way for some time – aware of each other's presence, but too burdened with their own thoughts to acknowledge it – until Su'la reached over and took My'ala's hand in her own, squeezing it gently like a pressed fruit.

"I had wondered if you'd be the one who'd come to find me out here," Su'la said, rolling a brass ring around her finger. "Did mother send you, by any chance?"

"She did, yes," My'ala replied. "For me to try and... *coax* you into getting some sleep soon. We do have another long day tomorrow, after all."

"That's true."

"And I do rather agree with her."

"Understandably, but... well." She let go of My'ala's hand and ran it through her hair. "If I'm honest, Mi, I've hardly slept… really… since we left Arbash."

The snake hissed in My'ala's stomach. "How come?"

"Because of all of *this*." Su'la gestured to the camp behind them, and the wider expanse of the desert beyond. "I've lived my entire life in a house, on a street, in a district, within thick walls overlooking the sea… and now I live nowhere, in a place of nothing, with nothing but *sand* all around me…" She sighed, catching her breath. "I'm just not adapting as well to it as I had hoped I would, is all. This is all so much more than I was expecting. It's a lot to take in… and I'm not the only one, as I'm sure you've already been able to tell."

My'ala frowned. "Do you mean about… father?"

"I do… and let me guess: when you asked why he was coughing, he blamed it on the desert air and having sand in his chest, and said sleep was the best medicine."

"I… yea." Her frown deepened. "How did you know…?"

"Because I've already had the same. He told me the *exact* same thing, when I asked why he was retching in pain and holding his chest." She scoffed. "And he's given that answer… because he loves you and I, and wants to protect us from the truth. He doesn't want to appear weak when we're both struggling as we are now…"

"But he *is* weak, and we can *see* that he's weak… so, why would he lie to us?" Her words came out pointedly, with an anger about how she had been deceived. "Why?"

"Because that's what he does — it's who he is," Su'la explained. "He's a strong man, and a protector. He loves us, and fears for us, and has to protect us no matter what. And now it's even more so since Dur'al…"

Her sister seemed to shrivel up as the name left her lips, and Su'la realised what she had been about to say. It was the first time any of them had ushered his name since the officer had delivered the news that fateful day, and something about it felt almost poisonous on the tongue. Sour and tired, and broken. They had hardly had the time or the strength to think of their brother before – and, thinking of the journey ahead, My'ala found it hard to think of when that opportunity would next be.

He's gone, she thought solemnly, hanging her head.

It's all gone.

"So what is father, sick?" My'ala exclaimed bitterly, giving in to the pain in her heart. "Has he got some… some festering wound that we don't know about? Are his days numbered? What isn't he telling us?"

"It's… more complicated than that," Su'la replied plainly, sensing her sister's frustration. "More complicated…"

"But why!" She ground her teeth. "How is it?"

"Because his *mind* is sick, Mi." She said it almost as an admittance, and produced a long sigh thereafter. "Since leaving the city, and going off with all these people into the Unknown… his mind has been too full for him to cope. He worries about us; he worries about the strain on you; he worries about our safety, and the other people we travel with. He worries about whether those who we've fled from are following us now, crossing the desert after us in the hopes of dragging us back in chains. He doesn't know who to trust, or where to go, or what to say… so he talks about desert air, and beetles, and pokes sticks into the fire in the hopes of it giving him some answers, even though he knows it never will."

"And now the effects of that are making him sick… *actually, visibly* sick," My'ala deduced. "Because his mind is weak…"

"…and so his body becomes weak too, yes."

"We should do something… we should help him."

"In an ideal world, yes, we should."

"Maybe I should talk to him, and… maybe I can tell him that I'm doing okay, and you're okay, and he has nothing to worry about. That we'll find a new home, and he can settle, and things can go back to normal—"

"And you would be lying to his face if you did so," Su'la interrupted, tapping her sister's cheek. "I'm sorry Mi, but you know you can't do that."

"But why not!"

"Because that isn't the *truth,* Mi! We don't know what comes next; we don't know what the desert holds for us. There are no guarantees in a place like this, and there's nothing you can promise. I can see it in your eyes… you know it's true, and that fact is eating away at you slowly, and you're not letting it go. Because you feel like the world is resting on your shoulders all the time, and you think you're the only one responsible for saving us—"

"I'm *fine,* Su'la," My'ala snapped, cutting through her words like a scythe. "This is about father now… not about me. He's the one suffering."

"Okay, okay… I understand." She lifted her hands in surrender before placing them on her knees. "You're right, this is about father." She paused, chewing over an idea, before meeting My'ala's gaze. "But if this ever does get too much, and you need someone to talk to… know that I'm always here for you, Mi. Always."

My'ala sensed her anger dissipate, mellowing like a warm bath. Her sister's pleasant eyes glinted at her, pearly gemstones in their sockets.

How could I ever be mad, when all you want is to help?

"I'm sorry, I… thank you, Su'la," she replied. "Thank you."

"We're very proud of you and what you're doing, Mi, please remember that. Because as much as father doesn't say it, and mother says it too much, and I don't always get the opportunity to… we are, all of us, proud of you." She placed a hand on My'ala's face and smiled. "You may not be the leader we were expecting in all this, or the one we would have necessarily chosen ourselves… but there isn't a single part of me that doubts the leader you've become. And that, I *can* promise you…"

My'ala took in a long breath, letting the cold air sweep over their faces, before she shuffled closer and embraced her sister under the growing twilight sky. As they embraced, an understanding passed between them – one of kin and blood, and so much more – that seemed to isolate them from the world for just one moment. Seconds became centuries; every heartbeat became an echo everlasting. And even when the parted, and sat opposite each other looking up at the stars, that same connection remained as if it had been there all along.

"Now, anyway, let's get back to the tent and get some sleep like you said," Su'la decreed, lifting to a stand and offering a hand to My'ala. "We have a long day ahead tomorrow, after all."

My'ala looked between the hand and her sister's eminent expression, letting the emotions and the fears wash through her, before she clasped Su'la's palm and lifted from the sand.

Ready for whatever the new day could bring.

II

THE MUSE

Stirring from a troubled sleep, My'ala awoke to the sound of scraping metal outside her family tent and immediately sat up, wiping her eyes with the balls of her hands. There were raised voices just beyond the walls of her sleeping compartment, engaged in an intense argument about something. Turning her head slowly to the right, she saw three large shadows projected against the outer cloth, with one of them making broad gestures with their hands. Craning her neck curiously, she squinted and tried to listen in on what they were saying.

"...*don't care what you have to say about it: she's only a girl, and she's sleeping, so it's best you leave her to rest before you bother her with any of your problems...*"

It was her father's voice, verging on a cough with each intake of breath. He sounded angry and tired, and whatever was going on clearly distressed him somewhat.

"We understand your concerns, sir, but his Highness has requested your daughter's presence immediately, and they will not be kept waiting..."

His Highness? My'ala thought, frowning. *What could he want?* She didn't recognise whoever it was that was speaking to her father outside, or why they had any kind of authority to carry out the God-Elect's orders.

Or why they want me so urgently, for that matter.

"Is that so? Well... if his Highness wants to see My'ala, then how about he comes over here himself and says that to my face?"

A grunt followed her father's challenge.

"As you wish," they replied.

Scanning the tent wall beside her, a fourth shadow joined the cluster of people suddenly, and My'ala's heart jumped in her chest. Studying the newcomer closely, she recognised the figure's thin frame and stout posture almost instantly, even through the tent cloth.

Is that...?

"I can apologise personally for the disturbance, my good sir," Aurelius said measuredly, *"and may I assure you that we would not be jeopardising My'ala's much-needed rest were it not for reasons of significant importance — as this, it turns out, may be."*

She sensed her father tense up outside, and watched him square his shoulders in the shadow of the tent like a dog with its heckles up.

My'ala gritted her teeth.

Oh no.

Before he could throw any more ill-placed remarks at the God-Elect, My'ala leapt out of her sleeping compartment and pushed the main tent cover open, emerging into a hazy, warm morning of yellows and blues and whites. Turning to her right, she took in the scene before her with a look of innocence that betrayed the rapid beats of her heart, holding an arm up to her brow to shield her eyes from the sun.

Ahead of her, her father — facing her now with an expression like chiselled stone — stood to one side with his back to the tent, regarding her silently with his teeth grinding in his mouth. The desert sun made him appear less weary than he had looked the previous night, but the redness in the whites of his eyes spoke of deeper, hidden pains still lingering just out of sight. Beyond him, she saw Aurelius stood with his hands behind his back, flanked by his two personal guards who remained just as intimidating and hard-faced as she remembered. The God-Elect had worn a rather morose look when My'ala had first emerged, but as their eyes met his face melted into a warm, relaxing smile — one that My'ala found herself returning, despite her father's damning glare.

"Is something wrong?" she asked politely, looking between the four of them in turn.

"No, nothing is wrong, Mi," her father replied. "I was just informing his *Highness* here that you could do with more time resting before being bothered with any more problems. The sun has only just fully risen, after all."

"I understand the concern." She turned to Aurelius. "Is the problem urgent?"

"We're unsure, but it's certainly unusual and may be quite important to us," the God-Elect replied. "I was hoping for your opinion on the situation before we proceed, but if you are wishing to rest longer as your father implies…"

"No, I'm ready," she said defiantly, nodding her head.

"Allow me to get dressed and see my mother, and then I'll be ready to depart."

Stood between them, her father closed his eyes and sighed, but said nothing.

"Excellent," Aurelius exclaimed. "Please, take what time you need and then we'll depart."

My'ala bowed her head. "Thank you, your Highness."

Turning, she stepped back into the main compartment of their tent and disappeared from sight – acknowledging another figure following close behind, shuffling into the shadows with a wheeze accompanying each step.

"Mi," her father said, almost like a whisper.

"Yes?" She turned to him then, looking over his complexion in the darkness of their tent, and saw how thread-bare his skin looked all of a sudden. His eyes were flitty and watchful, never quite focusing on any one thing. "What is it, da?"

"You really should rest… you know. You really should."

"I understand your concern, da, but… this is part of what I do now. There will be time to rest at a later date, I'm sure."

"I know, I know… it's just, you're always being dragged away to do these things, Mi, and I know it must weigh on you and tire you out. I'm only trying to look out for you."

"I know that, da." She took a step forward and hugged him, pressing her head into the dip of his collar. "And I never want you to stop looking out for me… but sometimes I have to do my own thing, too. That's just how things are now…"

Stood like a statue, her father said nothing in response, choosing instead to wrap his arms around his youngest daughter and hold her close for a moment. He held her close and tight, resting his chin on her head. She heard the steady beats of his heart in his chest, and the laboured rasps of his breath in his

lungs. It was a fragile moment, filled with words left unsaid —
for better or for worse, she wasn't sure. But as they parted,
and she looked up to his eyes, her father could only manage a
weak half-smile, like a bow never releasing its arrow.

"Good luck," he said eventually, stepping past her and
pulling the entrance to his quarters open. "We'll be here if you
need us... *whenever* that may be..."

With the fake smile slipping from his face, her father stepped
into his sleeping quarters and pulled the flap closed at his back,
leaving My'ala stood alone on her now-unsteady feet.

Thanks, she replied, taking a quick breath.

The snake in her stomach rattled its tail.

Accompanied by Aurelius and his guards, My'ala travelled east
through their makeshift camp sometime after, snaking her way
between the tents and ashen fires as the sun beat down over
their heads. The camp, never stationary for more than a turn,
was once again in motion as they passed through, with people
deconstructing their communal tents and covering their fires in
sand.

It had become part of their way of life over the previous few
weeks, cathartically unloading and repacking their gear as they
travelled and set down elsewhere, covering their fire-pits and
scattering the ash so as to leave no signs of where they had been.
They lived a nomadic existence, which proved an entirely
foreign concept to many of them, having lived within Arbash's
walled confines for a dozen generations at least, enjoying their
permanent dwellings and regular markets with places to work
and eat on every corner. But those were familiarities that had

been completely undone once they had set out into the desert, moving a kingdom's worth of materiel each day and building it up again by night. There was no permanence to their lives anymore, and little sense of structure – but the people of Arbash seemed to prevail nonetheless, taking comfort in the regimen of travelling and packing, until the intricate folds and binds of their tents were almost second-nature to them, and the civilian comforts of city life were little more than a cautious memory.

"They are a stoic people," Aurelius said, as they passed the last of the tents at the eastern edge of the camp. "I admire their courage, especially at times such as this…"

Under the canopy next to them, a young girl stepped out in a faded blue dress and gawped up at them with big, expressive eyes, stretching her arm out to wave with her mouth hanging aghast like a cavern. Smiling, Aurelius held his hand out and bowed his head in return, making the little girl giggle and stamp her feet in excitement, grinning ear-to-ear.

"We grew up on stories of hard times and overcoming our fears," My'ala said, waving to the little girl as they went past. Looking on inquisitively, the little girl managed a small wave in reply, before her mother called her name from within their family tent and she disappeared inside in a flash of pale blue. "Our ancestors were once desert nomads, after all. It's a big part of our history."

"Indeed it is. I remember the stories I was told about the first desert wanderers coming to Arbash, travelling across the sands to spy a beautiful valley on the edge of the World. They were truly magical tales."

"And now, out here, all we do is live those same stories for ourselves, and tell them to our children to remind us of our own strength."

"That's very true."

"I mean, if the desert wanderers of old could traverse this land once upon a time… then why can't we now?"

"Precisely so, yes," Aurelius agreed, nodding his head. He looked up the sandbank ahead. "And I suppose that's part of the reason I've brought you out here this morning, too."

My'ala furrowed her brow. "What do you mean by that?"

The God-Elect just smiled, and gestured to the crest of the dune beyond. "You'll have to see for yourself."

Oh… okay, she thought, pulling her robes tight about her legs as the God-Elect lead the way. She followed him up the dune-side with a wide, ambling gait, trying to disturb as little of the sand as possible, knowing that if the sand slipped away she could tumble and be buried in an instant.

Reaching the peak of the dune, she looked out on the sprawling landscape beyond and found it to be no different than any other patch of desert they had found so far. There were flat stretches of sandstone and grit, interspersed with meandering dunes as tall as mountains. Many of them wove in and out of each other and broke away in places, sliced open with great clefts as if the gods had gone at them with a knife. They stretched on into the impossible distance, an endless expanse as far as she could see until the sky and the horizon met in a haze of white and grey, and the Unknown slipped from view once again.

But that was not what garnered My'ala's attention as she stood swaying atop the crest of the dune. Her thoughts – and her sudden feelings of confusion and disbelief – were focused much closer to them instead, as she traced the curve of the dune down to a flat stretch of ground several hundred strides away.

Where a tiny, solitary tent sat nestled beneath a prickly bush, adjacent to the round stone shape of a very ancient well.

"A *well?*" My'ala said aloud, frowning intensely. "Out here?"

"Apparently so… and with someone guarding it, it seems," Aurelius replied, gesturing to the tent under the shade of the bush.

"But… why would they construct a well all the way out here, where there's no food source? It's hardly a feasible place to settle. Is it a stopping place for travellers, perhaps, or a relic of something long ago?"

"We aren't exactly sure of what its purpose is at the moment… or who occupies that tent for that matter." The God-Elect paused. "Although, that isn't even the strangest thing about this well."

"What is?"

"Well… probably the fact that it wasn't *there* yesterday."

My'ala turned to him. "What do you mean it *wasn't there?*"

"My scouts surveyed the area surrounding our camp before dusk yesterday, to see if it was suitable to make camp, and they found nothing but sand and dust in the immediate vicinity. And yet, when they got up this morning to check our perimeter again… this well had appeared, supposedly out of thin air."

"But that's… could the scouts have missed it the first time around?"

"It's unlikely: it's hard to miss something so distinct in a place that's near-enough the same colour, My'ala," Aurelius admitted, pulling a hand through his blonde hair. "Especially a structure of dark stone like that well is."

"How is it possible, though, that it just appeared out of nowhere?"

"We aren't sure." He sighed weightily. "It seemed entirely implausible at first – things don't just *appear* in a place like this as you say – but then I remembered something that you said to me several nights ago, and it got me thinking."

"What was that?" My'ala asked.

"You said about the old hermit you met, out by the ancient tree in the fields… Artemis, was it?"

My'ala nodded, pressing a hand against her abdomen.

"And I remember you telling me that, after you had spoken to him of an evening, he almost seemed to… *disappear,* as if he'd blown away with the wind. Is that correct?"

As she tried to subdue the pain in her stomach, My'ala acknowledged just how impressive it was that the God-Elect had remembered such a small detail from their prior exchanges.

And that he believes me at all, for that matter, she scoffed. *It's not every day that someone comes to you and says that they used to talk to a disappearing hermit with stars in his eyes.*

Although, what he says about this well does sound awfully similar…

"That's right, yea," My'ala clarified, catching his eye. "And from that, I guess you think this well – and whoever's in that tent – are connected to Artemis in some way?"

"It's just an idea… but it's the only idea I have for something that shouldn't be remotely possible," Aurelius explained. "And that's why I wanted you to come out here straight away, before the rest of the citizens are packed up and ready to depart. Because if they get to that well before us, and there *is* someone in that tent… then who knows what might happen."

"And as I have the most experience with '*disappearing things and unusual people*', you want me to make first contact?"

A redness formed on the God-Elect's pale cheeks. "I didn't mean any disrespect by making the suggestion, I assure you..."

"I know, I know, I'm only messing with you." My'ala nudged his arm with a smile, and a wave of relief came over Aurelius that sagged across his shoulders.

He let out a long breath. "So, would you be willing to make first contact, and see what's down there...?"

My'ala peered down at the tent and the prickly bush beneath them, a quiet resolve forming across her face. Investigating the well had the potential to be very dangerous, she knew, and she would have no back-up in the event that things got messy.

But that's what I'm here to do, My'ala proclaimed, standing a bit straighter. *I'm here to take the necessary risks.*

People depend on it, after all.

"I'll do it," she said simply. "I'll see what the situation is."

"Thank you, My'ala," Aurelius replied. "We'll be stationed on this ridge while you investigate, and if anything happens we'll be there to intervene as soon as possible."

"I appreciate it, thank you."

Plucking up a level of courage, My'ala took three long steps down the sandbank before she stopped suddenly.

"My'ala, what is it?" the God-Elect asked.

"I just... don't tell my father about this, please. He doesn't need to..." Her words caught on her tongue; she squared her jaw. "Just, don't say anything."

"You have my word." Aurelius bowed his head, wearing a grave expression. "The best of luck to you, My'ala."

She smiled and turned away in silence, a nausea churning in her stomach as she took another few shaky steps – wondering who she was about to meet all the while, and what kind of trouble she had just gotten herself into.

*

Approaching the well from the south, a cold wind pulled up My'ala's back as she walked and swept across the sandstone at her feet. She took a deep breath suddenly, startled by the shift in the weather, and tried to steady her racing heart that thundered in her chest. After spending so much time out on the dunes – accompanied by the ever-shifting sands of the desert – the feeling of solid ground beneath her boots was oddly relaxing and calm. If she closed her eyes, she could almost envisage herself walking along the promenades of Arbash, looking around at the flat-roofed houses and the distant heights of the valley cliffs. Inhaling the scents of spiced fruits and flatbreads drifting from market stalls. Smiling and waving at passers-by, who stood adorned in their finest coloured robes.

It was a fleeting memory, beautiful but never destined to last, as another gust of wind pulled at My'ala's robes and threw dust up into her face, dragging her back to a reality she had been trying to avoid.

And it was a reality that got suddenly much worse.

The sand whipped across her face like a slap, lining her lips and salting her tongue. Howling wind caught in her ears, whistling around her body. She was pummelled from every angle, struggling to stay upright suddenly like a cactus in a storm.

What's going on!

Coughing as the dust filled her chest, she peeled her eyes open and wiped them with the back of her hand. The air around her seemed to be consumed with sand, blotting out the hazy blue sky and the pearly white sun high above them. Everything swirled around her like a powerful vortex, darkening at the edges of her vision to make breathing almost impossible. For a brief moment, she wondered if it was the well's doing: if it was in fact some accursed thing deep in the desert, drawing nomads into its trap with promises of fresh water. Or maybe it was caused by the owner of the tent stood adjacent to it, conjuring the wind with some dark magic in an effort to turn her away.

My'ala didn't know the truth of it, and could hardly think besides – and in that moment of absolute fear, she felt as if she would never find out again.

Until the wall of dust fell away all of a sudden, clearing her vision and refilling the air in her chest, opening up the flat land ahead of her——

Where a figure in deep green robes stepped out from the orifice of the tent, and looked upon her with a twinkle in their single shimmering eye.

My'ala stumbled backwards for a moment, caught between standing still and running for her life. Something heavy lay across her shoulders like an anvil as she studied the figure opposite her: a woman with silky brown hair and pale, angular features, stood watching her in silence. Her robes folded in on each other many times with thin gold threads laced between. Tiny gemstones were dotted along a broach at her neck, and her single eye on the right side of her face shone with an otherworldly lustre, as if gazing directly into the heart of the sun.

My'ala was transfixed by her presence, and found herself frozen to the spot. Her breath caught in her throat and her eyes refused to blink, kicking up a flight response in her chest that she wished desperately to obey. She was locked in place, her limbs acting entirely against her will – and she could do nothing as the woman took several elegant steps forward and stopped just opposite her, tilting her mouth up to form a quiet and effortless smile.

"Hello, my dear," the woman said soothingly, her voice like a bubbling spring. "I've been expecting you."

Expecting… me? My'ala opened her mouth to speak, but the words appeared to dry up in her throat. Her skin crawled with anticipation suddenly; the desert seemed to tilt on its axis. "How did… who…?"

"I had a dream, you know… of a man with the stars in his eyes, sat beneath an ever-living tree. He said to me that a girl would come – a young soul, such a dainty thing – and that when she came, she would carry with her the burden of a thousand souls, destined for a new place to call home." The woman smirked, and twisted a strand of hair around her thin finger. "And, although I'm unsure of a great many things in this long and yet-so-fleeting life, Artemis was right about one thing…" She placed a hand on My'ala's cheek. "You are indeed such a young soul."

"You knew Artemis?" My'ala gasped. *Why did he never tell me about you?*

"I knew *of* him, my dear… it was no great betrayal that he never mentioned me," the woman replied, almost reading her thoughts. "I knew him towards the end of his time in this realm, through my dreams. He would come to me in my sleep with warnings and omens… and then, in his final conversation with me, he mentioned a young girl who would come from the west, destined for a sanctuary as yet unknown. And, as I behold here and now… on that account, he was correct."

"He knew I'd find you…"

She smiled. "No, my dear: he knew we'd find *each other*."

My'ala nodded, trying to understand. Artemis had guided her from Arbash's walls, out into the desert to find a new home and save her people from certain death. There, by an ancient well, she happened upon a woman who, by some immeasurable power that My'ala could hardly comprehend, had been contacted through her dreams by Artemis to warn her of their arrival. After that point, their paths – and their fates – had intertwined, until finding each other became inevitable.

Ever since I set out from Arbash's gates, I was destined to come here and find this woman, My'ala thought in disbelief, *and Artemis had planned it all along.*

But… why? She looked up and caught the woman's shimmering eye once again. *Why did he lead me here? What purpose does this woman serve in our journey?*

Why have we found each other at all?

"Why are you here?" My'ala asked, not knowing what else to say as she began to unravel what was going on. "Why are you here, by this well, in the middle of the desert… alone?"

Opposite her in peaceful silence, the woman seemed to consider her question for some time, before drawing a deep breath and clasping her hands together. "I am here, by this well, in the middle of the desert, alone… for the exact same reason that you and your people are here, out in the desert, camped on the sands with nowhere to go."

"We're looking for a place to call home."

"And I, my dear, am looking for what it means to *call* a place home…" the woman explained. Tilting her head, she turned east, gesturing out to the sands beyond. "As far as I understand it, you and your people have lived within the same walls for your entire lives – the same as your forebears, and their forebears, for generations past. You have lived in peace, and general luxury, with everything you could have ever needed for as long as you can remember. And it's a beautiful thing, I assure you… I'm rather jealous, I must say." She pointed off into the vague distance, studying My'ala's face as she did so. "But out here, things are different. Less certain. *Volatile,* almost. And out there… *somewhere*… there will be a place that could one day be your new home, and give you the same peace and luxury that Arbash once did. There are quite a few contenders, in fact, from my own experience travelling these lands… there are several different potential places for your people to settle down, and begin again as the ancient Prophets once did in your homeland." The woman stepped in front of her suddenly. "But that then begs the question: what does that look like in reality? I mean, *really* look like? And I'm not just talking about the physical things, either. There will be markets and vendors and herbalists, of course, and all the wonderful things you can recall from your old city… but what about the essence of the place, and the little indescribable things that make somewhere home? What does that truth look like, for you and your people?" She leaned in closer. "What does home really *feel* like, at its core?"

My'ala shrunk away from the strange desert woman, deciphering her curiosity. "You're asking me… what we should look for in life, out here… is that it?" My'ala deduced. "Is that what you mean?"

"In a way, yes, it is… because if I asked you that question, here and now, about what you're really looking for out here… you can't answer it, can you?"

My'ala frowned, balking at the statement in quiet disbelief. *What does she mean that I can't answer it? Surely that's ridiculous…*

With the wind circling over the dusty ground at her feet,

My'ala thought long and hard on the question she had been asked — arduously, for several moments — and realised, with a sharp intake of breath, that—

She's right. The ground seemed to open beneath her.

But… why?

Thinking on it again, she found she still had no answer — and the home that she would one day find and build with her people, was in fact without a definition.

She saw parts of it in her imagination: physical elements, like houses and fresh water and market stalls selling spiced fruits and flatbreads. She smelt parts of it, too: the stalls in the markets and the fragrances of the bathing houses drawing saliva in her mouth with temptation. They were all happy memories, and comfortable recollections of what her life had been before — but what that *was* exactly, and what made it so at its core, was entirely beyond her.

My'ala blinked slowly, her mouth agape, and watched as the desert before her seemed to tilt on its axis once again. As if everything was mishappen, and out of line. The woman's eye seemed to shine that much brighter next to her, inquisitive and lingering, deciphering her thoughts as they rose within her. But there was only one conclusion that came to her in that fragile moment, thinking on her past and the path ahead.

"You're right," My'ala murmured, her lips barely parting. "I don't *know*…"

The woman nodded slowly next to her, lifting her shoulders in a shrug. "And that's okay, my dear… you're allowed not to know. It's not something we are often forced to face, or consider."

"Artemis told me of the meaning of life… not what we should be looking for *in it*," My'ala explained, feeling a rise of bitterness in her chest. "He didn't prepare me for this at all."

"He didn't know."

"But he knew the enemy would come to our walls, and that we'd have to abandon our home when they did… he knew we would be out here with no guidance, and no idea where we should be going. We don't even know what we're looking for… he didn't tell me a *thing!*"

"There's no way anyone could have predicted something like this, or the problems you're facing now going forward," the woman said calmly, holding her stance. "Not you… not your leader… not even Artemis, in all his eminent wisdom. This isn't something you can plan for… it's just something that happens."

"But I didn't ask for this… for *any* of this."

"No-one does, my dear, no-one does… and I'm sorry." The woman released a long sigh. "When Artemis contacted me through my dreams, and told me that you and your people would be coming… he did it because he wanted to look out for you, and protect you. And, having spoken to him several times, the thing that I was most taken aback by in his last message to me, was just how… *afraid* he sounded. He *feared* for you, and for your people, and worried about your journey ahead. He feared what would come next, and that he would be unable to help when things got tough. And, even though I didn't know him for very long… from that last moment that he spoke to me, I knew one thing for certain." She paused, catching My'ala's gaze. "That he cared about you, more than anything else in this world… and would do anything to make sure that you'd be okay."

My'ala recalled the old hermit's wizened face and gnarled hands, and the glossy sheen over his eyes like two mystical orbs. She was reminded of his calm words, and his undying patience with her over the years, and the balance he always brought to her wayward, anxious soul. It brought a tear to her eye: a tiny crescent shape that curled over cheek and absorbed into the dust lining her skin. The memory rising and falling like a tide under an archway, in a place she had once called home.

I should be grateful now, rather than question what else could have been done: if it wasn't for Artemis, I wouldn't be here, now, with my family and my life. She recalled the starry night sky then, and the clusters of stars that had formed his familiar face. *He did every-thing he could for me, and for us as a whole… and even now that he's passed from this world…*

He still watches on from the stars.

"So, what happens now?" My'ala asked, wiping her eye with the cuff of her sleeve, reminiscing old stories like a bird spying its nest.

"The only thing that can happen, my dear," the woman replied, gazing off into the Unknown. "We press on, search for signs of life, and see if we can answer this question of ours. There's a lot to do, after all, and we best get on with it as soon as we can…"

"Wait… 'we'?"

Despite her still and measured expression, My'ala saw the remnants of a smile curling up the woman's cheek. "Come along now… you didn't think I would posit such a big question and just leave you to fend for yourself, did you?"

"Well, no, but I…"

"It was Artemis' last wish, my dear: that I would take up his mantel, and go forth with you into the desert in search of a place to call home. It only seems right that I honour that, now that you've made it here."

My'ala thought back to her final conversation with the hermit under the tree. "But… why?" she asked. "Why would his request matter to you? You don't even know who we are."

"Because, in this long and yet-so-fleeting life, there are many uncertainties that we face, and things that we can't control. But fulfilling a wise man's last wish, and helping those in need… now *that* is a certainty I can control. And I intend to, until my wistful final breath." The wanderer paused, and then grinned wickedly. "Besides, I quite like your gutsiness and guile, my dear… it almost reminds me of myself."

Even with the weight of the world on her shoulders, and a daunting task ahead of her, the woman's words brought a laugh to My'ala's lips that she couldn't help but let out. It cracked between her lips, and rippled from her mouth, and alighted something wonderful in her soul.

A something that had once seemed hopeless, and did not seem so bad anymore.

"Thank you," My'ala said. "Your kindness is really appreciated, especially at a time like this."

"Think nothing of it, my dear… it's my pleasure." She turned from her with a wink and looked off to the dune behind them. "Anyway, I think it's about time that I made my introductions and we made our move, wouldn't you say?"

"Yes, of course, I agree… um…" My'ala went for a name, something to refer to her by, but realised she had never asked the question in the first place. A redness rose on her cheeks, showcasing her embarrassment.

"What's wrong, my dear?" the woman asked.

"I'm sorry, I… I never got your name. I know I should have asked sooner…"

"Oh my dear, it's no problem – there's no need to fret." The woman smiled. "My name is Othella the Muse, but you can just call me Othella," she introduced, bowing her head. "And it's been a pleasure to make your acquaintance, My'ala. I think you and I will get on rather well… don't you?"

She turned and walked away with a smirk, striding elegantly across the sandstone flats toward the dune in the distance, where the white-red robes of the God-Elect could just be seen against the glare of the sun.

My'ala, fastened to the spot for what felt like an age, was left to ponder Othella's response at length, watching as the woman's green robes billowed in the wind and her hair flushed out against the sun.

"*How did you know my name…?*" she whispered aloud – but even as the words left her mouth, a smile started forming on her face, as she realised that she already knew the answer.

Artemis…

Of course.

III

THE NEWCOMER

With the camp in motion once more – heading out over the dunes of the Unknown like an industrious brood of ants – My'ala led from the front of the procession with Aurelius' scouts milling about in the distance, searching ahead for signs of trouble or the enticing prospect of life. The landscape remained largely unchanged, rising and falling in great sandbanks that wove like serpents to the horizon. It was a calm monotony, much like it had been for over a week gone past, and it allowed some time for My'ala to think on what had happened earlier that morning.

And the newcomer who now walks among us.

With a cautious optimism and a spring in her step, My'ala had introduced Othella to the God-Elect at the eastern edge of their camp, forever conscious of the guards and their spears stationed to either side. Aurelius had been very tense at first, regarding the strange woman and her starlit eye with a troubled stare, unsure of what to make of her. It was unusual to find anyone out in the desert wastes, let alone someone as strange and mysterious as the woman in her green robes.

Nonetheless, My'ala had done her level best to explain Othella's situation to him, and her purpose in joining their caravan on the long journey ahead. Aurelius had listened patiently, and asked his questions, and – helped by the Muse's unmatched charm and elegance – My'ala's hard work seemed to have paid off: the God-Elect had agreed to let the woman join them and travel with them into the Unknown, but only on the understanding that she would always be watched, and had to pull her weight as everyone else did.

Seemingly satisfied with the arrangement, Othella had bowed her head and blown a kiss to the guards, thanking Aurelius for his hospitality. After that, she had proceeded to glide off down the sand-slope at their backs and start introducing herself to the citizens, helping them load up baskets and lift goods onto the backs of their carts – possessing a casual indifference to the situation that was much to the God-Elect's chagrin.

Watching it as it had happened, My'ala had sucked in a troubled breath and thought that that would have been the end of the Muse's luck, and that her care-free attitude to keeping the peace amongst the citizens would have cost her her one chance to join them. But, after the camp had been fully packed and the people of Arbash had made their departure, My'ala had watched in awe as Othella assimilated with the crowds almost perfectly, as if she had been there all along. Men and women came to her with requests for assistance; elderly citizens told her stories from the backs of their camel-drawn carts; younger people came to her with questions, hoping to learn, as Othella talked of the stars and the sands and the vastness of the world around them. In the space of a morning, Othella had woven herself amongst the people of Arbash like a thread in a great tapestry, lacing new colours into an old fabric that had dulled after so many days of toil.

And even then, as she looked behind her with the sun directly overhead, My'ala caught the glint of Othella's shimmering eye as she navigated through the crowds, watching her help an older woman burdened with a very heavy cloth sack. The Muse hefted it over her arm and the lady gestured her open appreciation, starting off on some story or other that Othella listened to with a smile.

It's like she's been here all along, My'ala thought, turning back to the peaks and troughs of the dunes ahead. *The people have taken to her fondly, which hopefully means the next part of our journey is that much easier.* She closed her eyes, acknowledging the stinging and aching in her feet – a sensation that was no-doubt shared with the other travellers at her back.

Gods, I hope so.

"She seems to be making good impressions," Aurelius said, appearing at her side suddenly. Since his introduction to the Muse, he had excused himself for a while and gone off to speak to his guards, most likely to assess the new risks of adding Othella to their number. By the fact the Muse had not been placed in chains and dragged behind the carts at the rear, My'ala assumed their assessment had not been too harsh.

"She is indeed," My'ala agreed, whispering a silent prayer. "She's a natural."

"Yes. Part of me was worried that her presence would cause

distress among the masses… but I am very glad to see those fears were unfounded."

"As you've said before, we're a stoic people."

He smiled as if wearing a mask, a gust of wind sliding up the sandbank beneath them. His teeth ground in his jaw as he chewed over a thought. "Is she similar to how Artemis was, would you say?"

My'ala was taken aback by the question, but said nothing of it. *Why would you want to know?* "She is actually the complete opposite to him, if you can believe it."

"Really? How so?"

"He was more quiet and reflective… as you would imagine a hermit to be, I suppose," she explained. "He would have been quite overwhelmed to be this involved with everyone… in nature as in life, he was always one to spend his time alone."

"Out of fear or out of choice?"

"Out of choice, I think… people would have misunderstood his intentions."

"He kept himself out of trouble… I can respect that."

Trouble? My'ala frowned at the insinuation. "And Othella *isn't* keeping herself out of trouble?"

The God-Elect maintained a blank expression, brushing dust from his robes. "She is… for now. She's caused no trouble as of yet."

"But you're still uncertain of her."

Aurelius sighed. "I'm uncertain of all new things that we encounter out here, whether they're mortal like us, or otherwise," he said. "Until I know someone's true intentions, it's hard to feel any real certainty about anything. Especially someone like her."

"And what do you deduce from *'someone like her'*?" My'ala

retorted. She knew her tone was accusatory and lacked the appropriate respect, but something within her didn't seem to care in that moment.

"Well, this Muse certainly *looks* the part of a desert wanderer, and *behaves* with good decorum… but even the prettiest serpents can have the sharpest fangs."

My'ala felt her own snake twist in her gut, and grimaced. "I don't understand, though: she has no reason to harm us, or lead us astray—"

"That we *know of.*"

"Artemis contacted her before the enemy came to our walls: he *chose* her to help us find our new sanctuary," My'ala exclaimed, agitated suddenly. "He spoke to her in her *dreams,* for gods' sake…"

"So she *says,*" Aurelius snapped. He stepped over the crest of the dune and scowled. "For all we know, that could all be a lie, or some act of desperation to keep herself alive. She was out here by herself without any food or water, after all. People like that don't always think rationally, or have good intentions."

"She isn't lying. She mentioned Artemis by name… she knew *my* name, without me even saying it."

"Perhaps she encountered Artemis out in the desert, before he came to Arbash? Or, perhaps she avoided my scouts on patrol, and eavesdropped on your family to learn of your name?"

"I… I don't… that *can't* be true…"

"It could be: you were pitched along the outskirts of our camp, with a concealed dune-crest on one side. Who's to say that she wasn't listening in?" He paused, wagging a finger. "Who's to say she isn't one of the *enemy* that drove us out of Arbash, sent into the desert to intercept us and lead us astray —

buying them just enough time to catch up with us, chains dangling in their hands…"

My'ala gasped. "That's preposterous!"

"Maybe it seems that way for now, My'ala… but that doesn't mean it's impossible."

Aurelius looked to her then, turning on her, scouring her face with pupils like pinpricks. There was something different about him, she saw: something questioning, and uneasy. His eyes had narrowed, and his skin seemed to crawl with activity. Sweat lined his forehead and pooled beneath his eyelids. It was a side of him that she hadn't witnessed before; an emotion she didn't realise he possessed.

Fear…

"Do not let the love and trust you had for your hermit friend blind you to the dangers of this newcomer," Aurelius grumbled, shaking his head. "She may be telling the truth, and her and Artemis be cut from the same cloth… but we as a people must make preparations for the alternative, and what could happen if it turns out that you're wrong…"

Without the words to respond, My'ala looked over her shoulder to spy the first of her people crest the dune behind them, starting the slow descent down the other side. They were slow and cautious, taking each step lightly for fear of shifting the ground and sweeping out everyone beneath them.

At the top of the sand-bank, My'ala spotted Othella helping the same old woman from before, holding her hand as she crested the dune and planted her feet down on the other side. Despite her caution, the old woman slipped moments later and the Muse reached out suddenly to catch her, pulling her at the waist to hold her steady as an anxious chuckle escaped the lady's lips. My'ala watched Othella mouth *'it's okay'* in response, accompanied with a reassuring smile.

Is what Aurelius said true? she thought, tensing her stomach as the snake rattled its tail. *Is she a friend… or is she actually dangerous? And how could I know either way? How can I tell whether it's all just a ruse?*

Should I have brought her here at all?

Lost in a trance of her thoughts, My'ala hardly registered as Othella spotted her and waved at her from afar. She wore a broad grin, her one eye shining like a star – but My'ala just stared off blankly into the distance, into the space between the land and sky.

Does she really want to help us, and show us the way? Does she really know where these sanctuaries are, that we may call home? Should we trust her at all, with any of this?

My'ala sighed, feeling welts form in her soul – in the near-distance, Othella lowered her hand with a frown.

I just don't know, she admitted solemnly.

Who is Othella the Muse really?

Ahead of her, she was alerted to the sound of stomping feet suddenly, and the clatter of chain-links against a pair of thick boots. Turning around – tearing herself away from her own thoughts – she saw one of the scouts approaching Aurelius at speed, waving his hands in greeting. The scout wore pale slacks and robes over their chest, covering their head in a long ream of cloth to shield them from the worst of the winds.

"Ho, good sir!" Aurelius bellowed, bowing his head. "You come bearing good news?"

The scout bowed in return. "We believe we've found something, your Highness… a watering hole of some sort, over the next ridge."

A watering hole? My'ala's heart leaped with shock.

The God-Elect produced a warm smile. "Excellent news, officer: we shall make for there at once."

The scout bowed once more, acknowledging My'ala with a glance before loping off over the next dune toward their new discovery. Aurelius then turned to My'ala and opened his hands out to the sun.

"It appears our prayers have been answered," he said pleasantly, turning back to the path ahead.

Yes… My'ala thought, following on behind their leader. *And let us hope this proves to be a good omen…*

And not just a curse in disguise.

IV

CLEAR WATERS

The watering hole that the scouts had discovered rested in the bowl of three large dunes, cupped against the earth as if held in a child's hands. The bed of rock beneath it was a deep, earthen colour, not too dissimilar to the cliffs that had risen up around Arbash; the surface of the rock was littered with a number of deep cracks and fissures, from which the water seemed to well up naturally in a spring. At first glance, the water appeared clean and entirely suitable to drink — a belief that was further strengthened by the presence of a withered reed-bed on the far side, above which a number of small insects buzzed through the air.

Like zealots approaching a shrine of pilgrimage, the people of Arbash descended on the watering hole in a great flock, prostrating themselves at the water's edge and drinking plentifully from its banks. Children and the elderly were funnelled to the front, where they splashed water over their faces and offered their prayers, watching as the waves pulled up over their knees. Their breeches were soon dripping with water, and their stomachs were full to bursting with the gritty, tepid liquid. But, in that moment, with many leagues at their backs and the prospect of a long rest ahead of them, there was not a soul among the people of Arbash who cared enough to worry. They had finally found their moment of relief.

They had found somewhere to settle at last.

Taking her place alongside them and stooping low to the water, My'ala squinted at the sun's reflection on the surface of the water ahead of her, watching the waves ripple across in neat, undulating lines. Reaching down to her side, she plucked one of three large canteens from her belt and plunged it into the water at her knees, watching her own waves flutter out. The chill sensation of liquid over her fingers made her shiver and smile; the canteen sucked the water in greedily, before the last of the bubbles emerged and My'ala resealed it with the stopper.

Turning, she passed the canteen to Su'la stood next to her, who looked out on the watering hole and the bed of dry reeds just beyond.

"Make sure father gets plenty," My'ala requested, wiping her hands together and watching the dust peel off her skin. "He needs it the most."

"I will, don't worry," her sister replied. "Be quick."

Su'la twisted on her heel and retreated from the banks of the watering hole, returning to the rocky perch their mother and father had found just beyond. She handed the canteen over to their father, who took a long, revitalising draw of water and let out a deep breath, tilting his head up toward the beating sun with his eyes closed.

Hopefully that helps in your recovery, da, My'ala thought with a sense of ease. *And hopefully we can settle here for a while so you may properly rest. I know you need it more than anyone.*

Turning back to the task at hand, My'ala unstopped the second canteen and dipped its neck beneath the surface, watching it fill just as quickly as the first before sealing it closed and returning it to her side.

Next to her, a mother and her son crouched down on the bank and started filling their own canteen: the mother guided the boy's hand to the water's surface delicately, explaining that there was a perfect angle where the canteen could be filled without disturbing the silty substance at the bottom. The little boy – perhaps too young to care about such intricacies – listened intently nonetheless, watching the bubbles rise from the canteen's top with a singular focus that only children possessed. And, once the canteen was full and the bubbles stopped rising, the mother pulled it away and lifted it to her son's mouth, tipping it gently against his lips – where it spilled slightly, trickling down the boy's chest as he giggled and wiped his mouth and told her that she was silly. In return, the mother smiled and stuck out her tongue.

Watching them both, My'ala couldn't help but smile too.

There's still so much hope, despite what we've been through, she thought, reaching for the third canteen at her waist. *People still take joy in the little things, and remember good times.*

Remembering our connections to the past… to help make the most of our present.

Almost absently, My'ala leaned forward and looked down into the water beneath her, where the waves had suddenly grown still. She saw there the reflection of a woman she hardly recognised, and yet knew so incredibly well: one with deep-set eyes of green and gold, with strong cheeks and a narrow jaw and dark sunspots across their nose. A woman with a measured stare, and an authority far beyond their actual age. A woman in the reflection of the water, staring up at a girl on the bank — or rather, a woman in the reflection of the water, staring at someone who had once been a girl, but had changed so much since the last time she'd looked.

I am a reflection of my own past… looking down on the reality of the present.

My'ala lifted a hand to her face and pressed her fingers against her cheek, tracing the grooves and marks across her skin like a baby drawing circles in sand. Something about it felt otherworldly, and yet so very real. Out there, in the middle of the desert, prostrated next to a watering hole, she appeared like a completely different person.

And yet I am still the same, in so many ways… I am still me, at my core.

She stopped for a moment, claimed by a realisation.

And even though I have travelled far and no longer know my own home… I am still the same person, here and now, as I have been all my life…

Glancing to her right, My'ala looked over the rows of people at the watering hole's bank to spy Othella sat against a sandbank just beyond, plying at something with her delicate fingers like a weaver and their loom.

Perhaps this connection I feel has something to do with the question Othella asked me earlier, My'ala wondered, unlatch-ing the third canteen from her waistband and returning her gaze to the waters below. *Perhaps what I'm looking for in life is actually staring me right in the face…*

Connecting my present self to the memories of my past.

She dipped the vessel below the surface, and watched her reflection ripple away.

I think I better pay her a visit.

Sometime later – after delivering the canteens, washing herself off in the watering hole, and helping to reconstruct their family tent – My'ala managed to sneak off for a short while to go and find Othella the Muse, who lurked somewhere on the far side of their encampment under the watchful eye of Aurelius.

Her parents had been quizzical at first, when she had asked to slip away for a while and return around sundown. Her mother had inquired about where she was going, and who she was hoping to see; her father had studied her face with clinical eyes, as if trying to decipher an answer from her expression. Caught between them both like a cornered animal, My'ala had decided to fabricate an answer rather than try and explain the truth, knowing that a lie would displease her parents but not draw out an argument.

"The God-Elect requested my presence… once we were settled here, and had refreshed ourselves with the water," she had said to the huffs and sighs of her father. "I won't be long, I promise. It's important."

Her mother – ever the diplomat – had responded on their behalf, telling her to be careful and ensure she was back by sundown. My'ala had given her thanks, embracing her mother with a smile before she skittered off, trying to swallow down the bitter taste of the lie on her tongue.

It's a necessary lie, though, My'ala admitted, looking back on their family tent as she approached the watering hole's banks. Under their canopy, she saw her father had resumed his usual position at the edge of a newly-built firepit, adjusting the teepee of sticks with a look of thunder on his face – a look that My'ala knew she had caused.

I know I've disappointed you, da, but I can live with that. She ran her tongue over her teeth, with the lie she had told burning across her gums. *With your beliefs – and your misconceptions – I know you aren't ready to hear the full truth. There's an imbalance between us that needs to be fixed first. And, because of that, I'd rather I suffered your disappointment with this than riled your anger... as much for your own health as it is for mine.* She sighed.

I don't think either of us could take that at the moment.

Navigating between clusters of people near the edge of the watering hole, My'ala sensed a great relief had overcome the people of Arbash since their arrival – a feeling that rubbed off on her as well, banishing some of the lingering pains in the pit of her stomach. There was a lightness in the air, and a calmness as people engaged in chores and activities that had been stolen from them when they had left their city's walls. There were men and women knelt at the water's edge washing their clothes on bronze racks, talking amongst themselves like old friends. There were figures in cowls wading out in the deeper areas, hefting spears in their hands in the hopes of finding small fish. There were even a number of children running through the water and splashing each other on the western bank: children who were likely too young to have ever experienced the cove and the sea back in Arbash, who now delighted in the pool of water like fox pups fresh out of the den. All around My'ala, a natural balance reformed as people reconnected with their old ways of life — ways of life that she had feared had been left behind when they had fled their home, but now seemed to rekindle themselves almost contagiously.

It's resilience, My'ala acknowledged with a smile. *And how beautiful it is to see.*

Reaching the eastern bank, My'ala passed the last few clusters of people and looked out on the old reed beds just ahead, grimacing at the clouds of bugs that swarmed above them. To her right, on the side of a large dune to the south, one of the God-Elect's personal guards sat with their spear across their lap, frowning into the sun from the shade of a makeshift canopy. They appeared quite uncomfortable on their perch, constantly readjusting as the sand shifted beneath their thighs and they struggled to remain seated. Through the visor of their helmet, they appeared to be watching something ahead of them, focused on the reed-beds where My'ala now stood. Exactly how they could see anything in a full suit of armour under the roaring heat of the sun, My'ala could hardly fathom, but she was impressed by their perseverance nonetheless.

They must be watching something important, she deduced, narrowing her eyes. My'ala turned back to the reed-bed opposite her, and after a few moments she started to approach them with a smirk.

Or watching someone, *perhaps…*

Approaching the tall green stems with their yellowing leaves, My'ala watched as the thick bed of vegetation shifted before her, almost like a mirage. The stems parted, folding at the edges slowly, and from within its mass Othella the Muse manifested before her very eyes, stepping out and pulling her hood down with an elegant flick of the wrists.

"That's quite a neat trick," My'ala said with a smile, bowing her head to the Muse. "You'll have to teach me someday."

"And you'll have to teach me how to get these troublesome guards off my back," Othella replied, glancing over to the dune on her left. "They're rather persistent."

"It's a precautionary measure, more than anything. Even though *I* understand your nature and why you're here… the God-Elect and his personnel are not so easily convinced."

"Well, if I may… you don't sound overly convinced your-self, my dear."

My'ala pulled a hand through her hair, trying to dispel the redness in her cheeks. "I am… I am convinced. I know the truth…"

"And yet you blush, like a young girl caught stealing sweets." Othella smiled. "You know, it's no great harm if you *are* slightly cautious of me. I mean, I was half-expecting to be dragged with you in chains, so this freedom – however *supervised* it may be – is a welcome relief."

"I wouldn't allow them to do that, whatever the case."

"Because you trust me?"

"Because I think it would be cruel, and you deserve some respect. I wouldn't quite go as far as calling it trust."

"But aren't trust and respect not one and the same?"

My'ala sighed, grinding her teeth in her jaw. "I just know what it's like to trust your judgement on someone… and watch it fall apart from the consequences," she admitted, as the image of her brother in his suit of armour flashed behind her eyes. She shuddered. "I don't want to risk that happening again… especially not with so much at stake."

Othella nodded, as the wind rustled the reeds. "Well, I know my words don't equate the value of my actions… but I assure you that I have no intention of harming your search for a new home, and will do everything I can to make sure your people are kept safe. You have my word on that."

"Thank you. I hope you prove to be right."

"As do I… or your disappointment will be the least of my problems."

At that, they both looked over to the guard on the dune, who had been joined by his comrade while the Muse had been talking. Both figures watched them intently, with their hands never lingering far from their spear-hafts.

So cautious and fearful, My'ala considered.

What could Aurelius really be afraid of?

"But anyway," Othella continued, pulling a strand of hair from her face, "what was it that you came over here for? Besides seeing my neat party trick, of course."

"I wanted to ask you something about what we should be looking for out here, and what makes a home… a *home*," My'ala explained. "Because… I think I may have an answer to your question, if you'll hear it. Or something as close to an answer as I can get."

Othella's shimmering eye seemed to brighten curiously. "I can't say I was expecting that. By all means, my dear… *elucidate* for me."

My'ala drew in a long breath. "What makes a place a home, I believe… is how it connects to our past – and, so far in our journey, that's not something that we've really had the chance to consider. Travelling out across the desert, and seeking out sanctuary in the Unknown… has meant that our understanding of home, and our… *society*, I guess you could say… are not at the front of our minds, because… well, we aren't nomads, and nothing about this reminds us of home. Our way of life is settled and embodied by routine, which is no real surprise as we've lived behind stone walls our entire lives." She gestured to the ground at her feet. "But, now that we're *here,* and we've *settled* a bit… I see some of that old routine and way of life returning to us. People are out washing their clothes and fishing and socialising and creating chores for themselves, just like they did back in Arbash. We're reconnecting with our pasts, almost by instinct… and I think that's quite telling of what we as a people are looking for in life. A place to call home… where we can act like we're still at our *old* home. Would you not agree?"

Listening intently, Othella smiled and nodded when My'ala finished, looking out over the waters to her right and the people of Arbash along its banks. Her robes billowed in the low winds; her eye shone with lustre, as the wheels turned over in her mind. The sun shone almost hypnotically above, as My'ala laced a tongue over her lips and found them parched.

After some time, the Muse turned back to her, with shadows falling over her pale face. Her lips parted, forming an answer on the end of her tongue—

"No."

My'ala blinked, stunned. "*What?*"

"I don't think you should be looking for connections to your past on your journey ahead… especially if you want to stay anywhere with any permanence."

"But… why not?"

"Because this isn't Arbash… and you aren't *citizens* any-more."

A weight pulled over My'ala's shoulders, as the snake rattled its tail in her stomach. "I don't understand," she muttered.

"The life you have known – and the comforts you had in Arbash – hold no sway out here, where life is tough and nothing is certain," Othella explained, opening her hand to the dozens of people at the water's edge. "What you see here in front of you… this isn't people connecting to their past. This isn't people reliving their time in Arbash. This is what happens when you take everything from people, march them across a desert for nights on end, and then land them at a place where they can settle and rest for a while. They aren't seeking a life they once had… they're seeking *comfort*, now that everything they know is gone."

My'ala swallowed shakily; the snake's tail rattled all the way up her spine.

"In many ways, comfort is a good thing," Othella continued. "It offers relief… it keeps communities together… it provides respite for those who may be struggling with the adjustment. It makes people happy, most of all, doing things that remind them of stability. Arbash was their comfort, of course… but it's the everyday things that truly *settle* a person."

"Which is what they're turning to now," My'ala mumbled.

"Exactly, yes."

"But… you make that sound like a bad thing. Is… is it a bad thing, for us?"

Othella opened her mouth to reply, but closed it again just as quickly, reconsidering her answer. "Comfort is never a bad thing… but as with many things in life, it requires a certain amount of… *moderation*. Too little comfort, and people start to really struggle… but give them too *much* comfort, and when change comes they will simply fall apart under the stress of it all. In Arbash, that disparity wasn't really noticeable, because people could always find ways to navigate trouble. But out here, in the desert, where survival is no guarantee…" She scoffed. "Comfort can quickly become dangerous."

Othella rolled her shoulders, looking on My'ala sympathetically. "You're doing your best, my dear... all of you are, given the circumstances. And in many ways, your answer to my question is correct: the past is a good indicator of what makes people happy and what makes a place homely. But *only* up to a certain point. People will seek comfort in life until every problem they face is just a gust of wind... but out in the desert, every gust of wind could mean a sandstorm on the horizon." Othella turned from My'ala, facing the reed-beds from which she had emerged. "And there's no amount of comfort that can save you from *that*..."

The Muse lowered her head, almost in mourning, and took a single step forward toward the long rushes of the reeds——

"Wait!" My'ala cried, reaching out desperately, her heart hammering against her ribs. "Wait, please..."

Othella stopped, and half-turned to face her. "What is it, my dear?"

"What can we do?" She pressed her hands against her thighs, trying to dispel the hissing in her chest. "What can I do to stop this happening? I want the people to be happy... but I don't want them to waste what we have here. I just want them to be okay..."

"They will be okay, don't worry: these things have a way of sorting themselves out," the Muse replied, keeping her voice level. "Besides, they will have to face that reality soon enough, whether they're ready to or not."

"Wha... what do you mean?"

In silence, she looked down to her feet, and scraped one of her boots on the damp earth there. "This was the water's edge when we arrived... I wonder where it'll be by tomorrow?"

Without a word more, Othella turned and stepped into the

bed of reeds, letting them fall in around her body as she disappeared from sight like a ghost. Her words echoed out behind
her for some time, coiling on the wind as it brushed past
My'ala's face, stinging her ears and her cheeks.

The water's going down, she acknowledged, pressing her foot
down into the wet sand to her left. *Seeking our comforts has made
us complacent of the truth: we have to be careful of how much we
take...*

She looked across the water to the children splashing on the
opposite bank, with their parents washing their clothes nearby.

...and how long it'll be until there's nothing left.

V

TROUBLED SKIES

As dusk fell that night, and the auburn rays of the dying sun slipped below the horizon, My'ala and her family received an invite from the God-Elect to attend a modest feast in his quarters, supposedly in celebration of their achievements out in the desert thus-far. Naturally, her parents were rather sceptical of the invite, and asked My'ala what kind of work she had been doing for the God-Elect to earn such a special privilege. And, knowing that she couldn't offer the full truth to them because of her previous lie that morning, My'ala responded with another story that omitted some of the finer details.

"I was helping with some scouting work… and was giving some advice on our current water situation," she half-lied, trying to hide the sweat on her brow. "And, now that I think about it, Aur… the *God-Elect* did mention that he would be rewarding my efforts, so I guess this is what he meant."

"But why are we included… in that?" her father grumbled, before breaking out in a spasm of coughs. "It isn't… our celebration."

"I have no idea." My'ala just shrugged. "But with the offer of a cooked meal after so many days on rations… it's hardly an offer we can refuse."

And so, with their questions answered and their stomachs rumbling, My'ala guided her family out from their communal tent and off toward the large canopy in the south, where the warm light of torches made the God-Elect's tent glow like a geode of amber.

Stepping through the entranceway – past the stern gaze of the armoured guards – My'ala and her family were greeted by a wide room of green linens and tarps. A long wooden table of woven branches ran down the middle, draped in finely-woven cloths and beads. A number of candles burning in glass jars had been set into the wood intricately, shining across the sage tent walls and the heavy slate placemats. Six flat stones had been dragged in at some point to form seats, too, laid equally on either side with feather cushions strapped on top of them.

At the far end of the table – on a slightly-raised seat with two spears crossed behind him – the God-Elect watched his guests come in with a pleasant smile, gesturing for them to sit and get comfortable. He had done away with the white-and-red robes and had replaced them with simple brown garbs, which folded neatly with gold buttons on his sternum. With his ringed hands placed on the table-top, he gave a small wave to My'ala as she entered, before gesturing to his right and introducing their other guest——

Othella? My'ala gasped, sensing a tension behind her as her father ground his heels into the dirt. Her heart stalled in her chest.

What...?

The Muse looked over to them with a pleasant smile, pulling her hair behind her ears in an innocent gesture. There was another emotion hidden behind her eyes, too, My'ala realised: something uneasy, and awkward.

What is she doing here? My'ala longed to shout, looking between Othella and Aurelius as the serpent coils tightened in her chest. *Why have we all been brought here at once? This doesn't make any sense.*

Why is this happening?

Without an answer forthcoming – and with a growing sense of dread in her mind – her family found their places at the long woven table, with My'ala positioning herself opposite Othella so as not to stir any questions.

But I don't understand, My'ala pleaded, breathing shallowly. The cushion beneath her did little to hide the discomfort of the rock she sat on. *My parents don't know that I know Othella. Aurelius knows that, too. So why has he brought us all here together? What can he possibly hope to achieve? I thought he didn't trust Othella any more than my parents do...*

I don't understand.

"Thank you all for coming here this evening, and joining us for a splendid – and albeit modest – feast," Aurelius introduced with his usual charm and effervescence. "I wanted to do this as an acknowledgement for everything we've achieved so far, and how well we've all done since leaving the walls of our home. I know that My'ala has been indispensable to me as an advisor since leaving Arbash, and has been a great help in keeping people motivated and on task." Aurelius turned to her and smiled. "Equally, I know that you, lady Busskar, have been an invaluable seamstress for the citizens and their clothes… and that you, master Busskar, have repaired a number of our carts that have been stranded on the dunes over the previous days. You both have my thanks for that contribution."

My'ala's mother smiled pleasantly with a redness in her cheeks – but her father, by contrast, simply lifted a hand and grunted aimlessly at the table in front of him.

"As well as this," Aurelius pressed on regardless, "we have our newcomer from the desert, Othella the Muse, to thank for directing us towards this watering hole and bringing much needed relief to the citizens of Arbash… and for *curtailing* our use of the water over the day in the hopes of saving it. Your advice on that has been indispensable."

As the words left the God-Elect's mouth, My'ala sensed her heart sink through the floor at her feet. *I told my parents I helped with the water situation… which means they now know I've lied, or they've realised that I already know Othella.*

Opposite her, the Muse peered down the table and mumbled an awkward greeting to the rest of her family. Her mother and Su'la tried their hardest to return the gesture, smiling and exchanging anecdotes—

While My'ala caught sight of her father glaring at her, his eyes like two black stones.

Oh no…

"Anyway, now that we've all introduced ourselves," the God-Elect bellowed with a smile, "I think it's time we get to the main event, wouldn't you say?"

With that, he raised his hands and clapped twice, and three servants emerged from the room behind his seat, carrying with them bronze platters of delicious steaming food. There were grilled lizards and spiced olives; there were flatbreads and an assortment of ground pastes; there were slices of rich-meat and sparrow-breast; there were clementines and berries and fruits. The platters were spread out along the middle column of the table, illuminated by the candles in their jars as the aromas swam in their nostrils and drew saliva on the tips of their tongues.

They distributed the food evenly, sampling every piece and not missing out on a morsel. It took little time at all for the platters to be cleared, and for each of them to bear plates full of tender, beautiful food that they picked at with their fingers, letting the oils and resins drip across their palms.

"This food is beautiful," Su'la remarked, licking her finger-tips before plucking up another olive. "Thank you, your Highness."

"It is wonderful," her mother added.

"You have our thanks," her father muttered between mouthfuls, his distaste not extending as far as his hunger.

"Please, it is the least I can do for such honoured guests," Aurelius replied, tearing at a piece of flatbread daintily and mopping up a sweet red paste. "I would offer such pleasantries to every citizen if I could… but I'm afraid I have not packed enough food to do so."

Othella smiled. "Well, it's a shame that isn't another one of my party tricks… ay, My'ala? We could all do with a bit more food every so often…"

My'ala stopped chewing and stared at her with big, fearful eyes. Sickness ballooned in her stomach.

Somewhere at the other end of the table, a curled fist smacked down against the table-top.

"That being said!" the God-Elect exclaimed a little too loudly. "We have had some luck retrieving a number of small fish from the deeper parts of the watering hole. It seems they like to hide away in the cracks where the water rises from."

"That's fortunate!" My'ala's mother blurted.

"It is, yes. We hope there may be more around, if we're lucky…"

"Have you checked in the reed-beds yet?" Su'la suggested, reaching across to clutch My'ala's hand. "I imagine they like the shade and shelter there."

"Not as of yet, no, but it's a good suggestion. I know Othella here has spent some time over there… so I imagine she knows more than *I* do." Aurelius hid little of his displeasure as he glanced over to the Muse. "Would I be correct?"

"There was nothing there as far as I could see," Othella replied curtly, taking another mouthful. "Just lots of insects, and maybe a couple of dragonflies."

"That's a shame——"

"That being said, I didn't have much time to look, if I'm honest. I was busy… catching up with…"

My'ala sucked her cheeks in and tightened her grip on Su'la's hand.

And opposite her, in one fatal motion, the Muse extended her finger and pointed at her.

"…with My'ala here. It was a rather nice catch-up… if I'm honest——"

The God-Elect lifted his hand out in front of him, lowering Othella's arm timidly. He pulled at his collar despite the cold wind pulling through the entranceway, a redness blushing his cheeks. "Well, I… well… has anyone tried the lizard yet?" He spluttered. "It's supposed to be very good. My cook has said it's the finest—"

"Your *Highness!*"

The words – loud and fury-laden – shook the air around them like the heat from a wildfire. My'ala's head swam, as she shrivelled up and longed to disappear.

With bated breath, all eyes turned to the far end of the table beyond—

Where My'ala's father rose from his seat, his jaw churning like a grindstone.

"May I ask you a question, *your Highness.*"

The God-Elect visibly tensed next to her, a bright sheen over his eyes. "Of course, master Busskar… of course."

With an accusing grimace, her father speared a finger out towards Othella. "I need a point clarified, if you *may*. Over the previous day, has my *daughter* – who has spent increasing amounts of time with *yourself* – spoken to this… *thing* we sit with… and *if* she has, were *you* the one who allowed it?"

My'ala tried to swallow, but found a wedge lodged in her throat; opposite her, Othella's eyes widened as she realised what was going on.

Between them, consigning defeat, the God-Elect lowered his head and closed his eyes, offering only a sigh.

"I'm sorry, My'ala…"

The air around her rippled suddenly; the candles flickered and spat.

My'ala turned to her father with tears in her eyes. "Da, please…"

"You *lied* to us?" he rasped through his teeth, the pain weeping from every pore across his body. "You went off on your own… and *lied* to us?"

"Da, I'm sorry, I had to… you wouldn't have liked the

truth——"

"No, we *wouldn't* have liked the truth, Mi!" His voice rose, with veins pulsing over his temples. "And do you know *why*? Because the truth was *dangerous,* and foolish. Why did you think it was a good idea to speak to this *thing* by yourself, hm?"

My'ala clenched her jaw, tears rolling over her face.

Her father opened his hands.

"Why*!*"

"*Because I was the one who was asked to meet her first*!" My'ala wailed, swatting Su'la's hand away and holding her face. "Why can't you just let me make my own *choices!*"

But, in that moment, her father didn't hear a word. He didn't even acknowledge her tears, or her silence. His attention – and his newfound rage – had been redirected else-where, as soon as the first words had left My'ala's mouth.

"*You,*" her father growled, curling his lip up at the God-Elect opposite. "You let her go to speak to this thing… by *herself? You* put her up to this?"

"My'ala has experience with people like her, and I made a *choice* as to the best course of action," Aurelius replied levelly, lifting his hands to stop the guards who had charged into the tent at the commotion. "So, if you are to blame anyone for what's happened, blame *me*… My'ala has done nothing wrong here——"

"I'll blame whoever I damn well want, you *child,*" her father spat, pointing a finger at him. "You put my little girl in danger, and you did it *knowingly.*" He placed a hand on his chest and scoffed. "And here we all were… thinking you were out here… to *protect* us…"

Othella lifted to a stand suddenly, turning towards him.

"I don't think that's very fair, you know——"

"I don't *care* what you *think!*" her father boomed, turning on the Muse with redness in his face. "I don't even *want* you here! I don't want you worrying my daughter, and stressing her out. She's going through enough, for damn's sake!"

He gritted his teeth, glaring at everyone across the table. The candles flashed violently. The wind howled outside.

"I want it to end! All of it!" The veins bulged in his neck. "I want you all… to leave… my girl *alone*. So… *why* can't you *all* just… *ju*…"

In the flickering light of the dining space, with shadows swirling across the tent walls, her father's face contorted like a knot of rope before their very eyes, as he clutched at his chest with clawing hands and swayed against the table. He rasped, his breath laboured and shuddering all of a sudden, before the light dimmed slightly in his eyes…

…and he collapsed to the floor, unmoving.

My'ala stared at the spot where her father had been standing, her mouth hanging agape.

She didn't hear her mother scream.

She didn't hear Othella gasp.

She didn't hear Aurelius bellow for his guards to assist.

My'ala stared at the spot where her father had been standing, her mouth hanging agape, and realised in her silence——

This is all my fault…

VI

DESPAIR

Morning arrived, sharp and bright, but nothing was the same anymore.

On the back of a canopied cart with the orange glow of dawn behind her, My'ala looked down on the unconscious form of her father's body, and a small pain emanated from her heart like the tiny prick of a needle. Almost in a trance, watching him closely, she reached for his hand and placed it in her own, clasping it gently against her palm. It was so fragile and soft, lined with bones and tiny veins like little pale rivers. She could feel his pulse rippling through his thumb: agitated and stuttering and not at all correct. Desperately, part of her wanted to squeeze his wrist, matching the rhythm of her own pulse in the hopes it would synchronise and get better, but she knew that something so simple could never work, and she'd be left just as heartbroken as before.

Because in the God-Elect's tent that night, her father had not died in the end – but, as she had watched on from the opposite side of the table, something inside My'ala had.

Something I'll never get back.

The God-Elect's personal guards had been quick to act when he had first collapsed, rushing in and checking his vital signs, watching the steady rise-and-fall of his chest. My'ala's mother had been hysterical, watching the guards perform their duties as Aurelius did his level best to comfort her, offering reassurances that he would be okay and that the best people were on hand to help.

Once her father had been deemed well enough to move, the guards had hooked their arms under his legs and shoulders and carried him out into the cold desert night, veering off to the right where the nearest baggage cart could be found. The guards had attempted to keep his body as level as possible, as Su'la charged ahead of them and reached the cart first, leaping up onto the cloth sacks to begin frantically clearing room. In no time at all, she had managed to level out a small area that would hold their father's body amongst the sacks like a nest.

Or like a tomb, My'ala had thought morbidly, as she watched them lower her father onto the cart and mould the sacks around his neck to keep him steady.

From there, much of the rest of the night had been something of a blur. My'ala recalled the guards tipping water into her father's mouth in the hopes he would be conscious enough to drink. She remembered Su'la's frantic hands as she began to erect a canopy above them. She remembered her mother's tired, teary face holding her own, saying that it would be okay over and over again as much to convince herself as it was to reassure her.

My'ala had been there to witness it all, and yet could hardly piece any of it together. It was all hazy and fragmented in her memory. At some point, the guards had stepped aside and declared their father to be stable, admitting that they were unsure what was wrong or when he would rise again. He had received some water, and his breathing was under control, but whether her father would open his eyes again or not, they truly could not say.

As they imparted the news, her mother had started crying again, and with Aurelius and Su'la holding her steady, she had sunk to her knees and wept. My'ala, meanwhile, had stumbled blindly towards the cart, climbing up onto the sacks to look upon the body of her father. She remembered losing her breath when she saw his sad, resolved complexion; she had started sobbing, when she then saw the tremors in his chest where his heart and his breath didn't meet. Lowering to her knees next to him, she had curled up on her side and placed his hand in her own, crying quietly to herself as she drifted into a troubled sleep.

And for the entire night, she had held his hand, refusing to let him go.

"I'm so sorry, da..." she whispered, clutching his hand tighter. Even with her stomach growling and aches racking her body, she refused to move or let her eyes wander from his absent, quiet face. "This is all my fault... this is all *my fault*..."

She lifted his hand to her face and kissed the back of his knuckles, trying to steady the convulsions that racked her body.

"I didn't know what to do, or what I should've said... it all got out of control so fast," she continued. "I never meant to lie to you… I never mean to lie at all. I just omitted parts of the truth — the parts you couldn't hear, or would refuse to understand — and… I thought that would work. I thought maybe I could… keep it hidden, or something… and not cause you the stress of having to know the full truth…" She sighed tiredly. "I shouldn't have done it, and I know that now. I should've faced the truth, and been honest with you, and I'm sorry." Lowering his hand — the hand that she had held all night and clasped so tightly that morning — My'ala rested it against her father's stomach, and gave it one final squeeze. "And now I can't even tell you that… because you're drifting, somewhere between this world and the next, and there's nothing I can do but wait, and pray…"

And hope…

From behind her, the near-silent sound of footsteps on loose sand caught in her ear, approaching the cart from the right. My'ala turned slowly, wiping stray tears from her cheeks, to see her sister appear from beyond the canopy, smiling meekly at My'ala as she rested against the cart's rear gate. Her eyes were red-rimmed and crusted with salt, much like My'ala's own.

"Hi, Mi," Su'la said softly, reaching out to hold her arm. "It's good to see you're awake. Are you keeping da company here?"

My'ala nodded slowly, glancing back at their father's absent face.

"That's good, that's good… you're the best person for it, Mi. How is he?"

"He's… he's okay." The word *'stable'* crossed My'ala's mind, but the thought of it made her shiver. "Breathing and… and his eyes flit sometimes when there's wind, or when I talk or touch his hand."

"Well, that's good! That's good news. It means he's still here, with us… with you, Mi." She smiled, opening her eyes out, and put on a comforting face so strong that My'ala found herself nearly in tears all over again. "He's listening to you, and he hears you."

"I just hope he'll be okay… and that he comes back to us. I need him… I need to tell him that I'm *sorry*…"

"And you will, in time." Su'la rubbed her thumb against her arm. "He'll come back, and he'll be here with us again, and you can say everything you need to. But for now, all he needs is rest, and time… and he needs you to carry on being strong, and doing what you can for these people. We all do, Mi."

My'ala took a deep breath, letting Su'la's words sink in, before she leaned forward on her knees and wrapped her arms around her sister, holding her close in a way that only siblings could. They embraced tightly; My'ala let her heart stutter, and her breathing pull tight into her chest. She let the tears fall, but did not sob, allowing them to spill down her face thoughtfully and dry into Su'la's blouse. The landscape before her seemed to shift and change, morphing before her eyes.

"I love you, Su'la," she mumbled. "Thank you."

"I love you too, Mi," she replied. "Always."

They pulled apart and managed to smile weakly, before Su'la adjusted her blouse and glanced over to her left.

"And I suppose that, as you've been here all night, that you haven't heard the news this morning?" she said.

My'ala looked puzzled. "What news is that?"

Rather than answering, Su'la offered her hand to My'ala, who took it and stepped down from the back of the cart shakily, landing in the soft sand with a splash of dust. Once she regained her balance, she frowned towards her sister, who gestured over to the watering hole nearby with a face like shattered glass. My'ala followed her direction, and let loose a gasp when she saw what Su'la was pointing at.

"It's... it's *gone*," My'ala muttered, staring in disbelief at the muddy-brown dirt that had once been the watering-hole's banks. Looking out further, a tiny, shimmering puddle was all that remained, just above the deep fissures that fed up from underground.

It's all gone...

"It happened overnight," Su'la explained, "and, as far as we're aware, we weren't the ones that caused it. No-one used the watering-hole after the curfew was given by the God-Elect yesterday, and the situation seemed to get better for a while... and yet, when we went to fetch our drinking water this morning, this is what we were greeted by."

"Is there no way of bringing the water up from underground?"

"The fissures are too narrow, and we don't know how much water is actually down there... it's not sustainable."

My'ala nodded, a well opening in her diaphragm. "So... does that mean...?"

"Yes, it does," Su'la finished with a sigh. "The God-Elect has already given his decree: we're to depart within the next few turns, and we will head out into the Unknown once more. Our time here is done, and the vastness of the desert awaits once more..." She breathed the words out in one long trail, almost exhausted by the idea of it, but soon righted herself with a stoic expression and smiled towards My'ala. "Come join us when you can, so we can help ma with packing her things – she's rather fragile, as I'm sure you can understand. Da will be safe here in the meantime: he's been put under the supervision of the God-Elect's guards, so nothing will happen. He's in good care."

She leaned over and kissed My'ala on the head, whispering a quiet prayer before brushing down her skirt and making off toward their family tent.

My'ala watched her go, knots pulling at her heart, her eyes following Su'la's path up to their tent where their mother busied herself with packing, fiddling with the canopy struts like a baby trying to unscrew a tap. Su'la was there moments later to help her out, and between them they managed to pull the cloth drape down and roll it neatly into a pack.

And like that, we have to move on again… abandoning a place that could have one day been our home, My'ala thought, breathing deeply. *Heading out into the Unknown once more, no closer to finding our answers…*

Left with so many questions, and so many things left unsaid.

She looked back to the enclosed cart, and the ridges of the cloth sacks where her father's body lay resting. A striking pain lanced through her stomach, hissing at her with unease.

With resignation on her face, she turned to their tent and left.

VII

FORGIVENESS

Expeditiously, like fledgling sparrows opening their wings to feel the breeze against their feathers, the people of Arbash abandoned the shelter of the watering hole and returned to the vastness of the Unknown, seeking the next distant place that they hoped to call home. Their time at the watering hole had offered much needed respite after so many days traversing the sands. It had allowed them to rest their tired muscles and their truly exhausted souls. They had drank from the waters and replenished their supplies; they had washed their bodies and cleaned their possessions. And, despite the fleeting nature of the whole affair, they remained resilient in the face of defeat, and looked out upon the eastern horizon with their hopes still very much intact.

They had packed up without fuss, and left the sun-bleached

banks of the watering hole without question that morning. Loading carts and sorting their supplies, they had gone about their tasks methodically with the same due diligence as ever. The fact that they were abandoning a place that could have been theirs forever, hardly seemed to bother them at all. As with all things in life – and all suffering they endured – the people of Arbash looked on the experience as yet another trial of their existence. They were nomads, now, after all: the desert had become their reluctant home, and its nature was far from certain. Good fortune would be hard to come by, and in turn could rarely last. Regardless of how long they had spent at the watering hole, they knew to count it as a blessing. Because the desert could be as fickle as it was incredibly vast.

And every cresting dune could fall away just as quickly.

And so it was, with the sun beating down over their heads and the scorching heat blistering their heels, that the people of Arbash set off into the Unknown once again, driven by a sheer determination to find the true place to call home, no matter the odds stacked against them. They did so with helping hands and kind smiles, and the open hearts of good humanity. They helped where they could, and prayed where they couldn't, and looked out on a white-blue horizon with long exhales of breath. Hoping to see forever out there.

Somewhere.

Anywhere.

Trailing at the rear of their nomadic caravan, with the churning wheels of the baggage carts rutting the sands just ahead, My'ala pulled her cowl further over her face and squinted against the brightness of the sun. The near-whiteness of their surroundings stung her eyes furiously, and the ripples of heat rising off the dunes played tricks with her mind.

Nothing stayed in focus for very long. The sky and the dunes merged together like silty water, with no definition forming in between. Every person ahead of her – stretching down into the valley between the sandbanks and up over the crest opposite her – was little more than a smudge of colour, as if someone had dappled the sands with tiny flecks of clay.

Trying to keep pace with the rest of her people, My'ala knew it would have been smarter to stick with her mother and Su'la amongst the crowds, where the closeness of everyone around her could act as a marker against the hazy intensity of the sun. On her own however, at the rear of the caravan with only the carts to steer her in the right direction, even a few moments' hesitation could leave her stranded with no means of knowing where to go. It was foolish, really, to put her life at risk with so little care.

But even so, I know I can't leave him, My'ala thought, with her eyes trained on a particular cart trawling over the sands to her right. *I have to be close… to make sure he's okay.*

Being near her father, who still remained unconscious under the canopy's cool shade, had numbed the stabbing pains in her heart, banishing the hiss of the snake that had made itself comfy in the pit of her chest. It tempered her thoughts, and stilled her breathing, and kept the rattle of the serpent's tail quiet. My'ala did not know what the snake wanted, or what it was trying to acknowledge with its presence in particular, but the imagined pain when it flashed its teeth was enough to set her on edge, and she sought her own solace wherever she could in an effort to keep it at bay.

It comes when I'm weak, and think too much, she interpreted, imagining its amber eyes and the scaly skin around its lips. *It tries to lure me in… to tempt me away from sense and reason when I need it most. I fight it off, and push it away whenever it comes.*

But one day I fear it may get too strong, and that I won't know what to do when it does.

She pondered the idea for several moments – allowing the snake to knot in her chest as she did – when she was drawn to the sound of trudging feet approaching her from the left suddenly, and My'ala turned to find Othella step in next to her with her green cowl wrapped tight about her face.

"Hello, my dear," the Muse said meekly, mirroring her steps.

"Hello," My'ala replied.

"May I… join you, and walk with you?" She spoke with a timidity that she hadn't before, testing the waters to see if My'ala would bite – *and after last night, she may be right to be cautious.* "Although I do of course understand if you want some… time alone…"

"You can stay," My'ala replied softly, as a thousand tiny emotions flickered behind her eyes. "You can be here, if you like. I don't care… I don't *mind*, I mean."

Othella nodded, but said nothing; My'ala scratched at her palms and took a long breath. They descended into a pit between two large dunes and started the task of ascending back up the other side.

"The wind has subsided today," Othella muttered, breaking the uneasy silence. "You can feel the sun more on your arms and face, can you not?"

"Yea… you can."

"Just as good we have our robes…"

"Yea."

"…to keep our… heads protected."

They fell to silence again, letting the low breeze speak for them. Tiny waves of dust skirted across the dune-side and nestled in the bindings of their old sandals. My'ala sensed a pressure building on the back of her head – stress, or the feeling of something impending – and lifted a hand to dig her fingers into the back of her skull—

"My'ala?"

She stopped. "Yea?"

"I want you to know that I'm sorry… for what happened in the tent last night," the Muse said softly, slowing her pace. "I am truly, truly sorry for it."

My'ala nodded absently in reply, a tension pulsing down the back of her neck. "I understand, I…" The sand seemed to swirl and melt beneath her, as if the ground intended to swallow her up. "I don't… I…" A disparaged breath escaped her lips. "I don't even know where to begin with it… *any* of it…"

"I… yes, I understand—"

"Why were you there?" My'ala asked, more forcefully than she had intended. "I mean… why were you at the table with us yesterday? Did you request to be there, or did Aurelius invite you?"

"I was invited, the same as you… and, like you, I was expecting to be there *alone*."

"So… you had no idea either."

"None at all. When I saw you and your family walk into that tent with us, I was as surprised to see you as you were to see me. I hadn't been told of any other guests… and I did wonder afterwards if it was exactly wise for the God-Elect to put all of us together in the same room like that."

"It was a *catastrophe*," My'ala said bluntly.

"Yes, in hindsight it was… but I don't think that was the God-Elect's intention – quite the opposite actually."

My'ala stood baffled, frowning. "*How?* How could that have gone any other way?"

"Because – if I may – I believe that the God-Elect invited us all there in the hopes of… *straightening things out* between the three of us and your family. To bridge a gap, and end any potential confrontation going forwards. After all, I'm sure all of your time spent with the God-Elect has raised some eyebrows from your parents?"

My'ala considered, and nodded. "Yes… it has."

"And, as I garnered from my *mishap* last night… your parents were completely unaware of your relationship with me?"

"It would have caused more harm to tell them the truth," she replied matter-of-factly, wincing at the hurt expression Othella made in response. "And that's purely because they wouldn't understand it as I do… it's nothing to do with you personally."

"I see," the Muse replied, throwing a cowl over her own emotions. "Well… that story does fit into my understanding of why the God-Elect invited us both to the feast last night, so at least there's that."

"And that understanding is…?"

"That he wanted to use the feast to establish a connection between us, so that you could continue speaking to me and talking about what we should be looking for out here, without it worrying your parents. To make everything less secretive, and less stressful." As her face darkened, Othella pursed her lips. "And I, without realising it, stuck my foot in it and ruined that plan completely…"

My'ala sensed the wind pick up around them suddenly, looking to the Muse with quiet, thoughtful eyes. Her assessment made sense, My'ala knew: the God-Elect *had* been trying to steady the waters by inviting them all to the feast at once, establishing connections that weren't there previously to take some of the heat off of My'ala's back. It served many purposes in that regard: it was a sign of good grace from Aurelius, to show that My'ala's leadership was being respected; it was a bonding exercise for Othella, to make their conversations less secretive. It was an olive branch, too, to her mother and father, in the hopes of making things better going forward.

And, through no fault of her own, Othella ruined it, My'ala thought, although the word 'ruin' put a bitter taste on her tongue.

No: Othella didn't do anything wrong. She was her normal self, trying to be as jovial as she could be: setting a tone that would have settled any tension under usual circumstances… but in this case made them so much worse.

My'ala looked ahead to the cart off to their right, where the thin cloth canopy billowed in the wind and the large wooden wheels drove deep trenches into the sand.

The blame for this… for what happened last night… is not Othella's for saying the truth, nor the God-Elect's for inviting us there in first place.

The blame is mine, and mine alone… for lying to the one man I should have trusted.

"Othella?"

The Muse turned to her, the radiance in her singular eye shining brightly. "Yes, my dear?"

"It's not your fault, y'know… for what happened last night."

She frowned, taken aback. "Are you sure?"

My'ala sighed, feeling the tiny marks of tears evaporate around her eyes. "You were trying to make things better… and the God-Elect was, too… but ultimately, before that feast happened, I failed to be honest with my father, and that's the reason that he's in the state he's in now." She rolled her thumb and finger together, watching the dust peel off of them. "It is my burden to carry, and my blame to bear."

My'ala felt her stomach knot, and a biting pain push into her abdomen. Tears continued to well in her eyes and dry out just as fast.

The Muse said nothing at first, giving My'ala space to breathe, before she stretched an arm out and touched her shoulder tentatively.

"Regardless of where blame lies, and who's at fault in this… I'm still incredibly sorry for what you have to suffer through now, and the weight that bears against your heart," Othella said, walking slowly. "I wouldn't wish that on anyone, and if there's anything I can do at all, please don't hesitate to ask."

My'ala reached up and clasped the wanderer's thin fingers, nestling them against her palm. A reflectiveness fell over her mind, like the rise of an eagle on the wind.

"Thank you… *thank you*," she replied, nodding her head and letting Othella's hand go, as something stitched over in her chest and the hissing in her stomach slipped away.

Stood at the base of the dunes with walls of sand all around her, My'ala took a long breath, and opened her lungs out once more. The breath was full and refreshing: fuller than any she had taken since the previous night. Expanding against her ribs; stretching her legs and filling out in her cheeks. Defying her tiredness and fatigue, so that when she next opened her eyes the rising sands seemed somewhat clearer.

Da would want me to be strong, in the face of my feelings, she thought, straightening her back. *People still need me, above all else.*

Time to do him proud.

VIII

NECESSITY

The day passed by without a whisper – endless, and eternal – and as the sun's orange orb touched the edge of the horizon, the people of Arbash held their hands up in prayer, safe in the knowledge that their travels could end and they could soon find a place to spend the night.

As sighs of relief passed amongst them, and they drank their rations of water however, the true consequences of their journey began to show, rising to the surface like a trapdoor spider. Their limbs were impossibly sore, addled with rashes and burns. Dust clogged their nostrils and collected under their eyes. Their stomachs growled and their lips cracked, desperate for a morsel of food. The heat and the light that had over-whelmed them that day swam across their vision painfully, until their heads pulsed with the rhythm of their heart and they struggled even to stand.

Children clung to their mothers' legs and rubbed at tired eyes. The elderly huddled together in frail congregations, trying desperately to stay upright. Cart handlers slumped against their seats, pressing their hands against their temples to stem the drumbeats within. All around, the people of Arbash began to understand the truth of the task at hand. For the path ahead was harsh and unruly.

And their survival was never certain.

So with dusk fast approaching, and the cold night air pulling in, the God-Elect's scouts loped off over the dunes and went about finding the next place to make camp, ascending every rise and descending again just as fast. They went about their duties diligently, and searched like a pack on the hunt – and as the sky became bronze, and the sun bled out in the west, their cries echoed out into the encroaching night sky, indicating they had found somewhere safe to rest until morning.

The people of Arbash flocked to the location, and wasted no time in building up their temporary home. Canopies were raised in a matter of moments. Tent posts were buried deep in the earth and wedged in place with stones. Carts were unloaded and food was handed out to any poor soul who needed it.

Fires were lit. Embers crackled, and tiny plumes of grey smoke dashed the auburn sky. The smell of burnt wood and charring grains floated through the air like a zephyr, as people settled down for evening meals to rest their weary bones.

The sky overhead burnt orange and crimson before the sun dipped out of view. Blues and purples merged along the horizons like silk reams, dancing with the winds. The sheer, beautiful blackness of night expanded high above them, dashed with tiny stars.

And beneath it all – sat alone on a sandbank with her parent's tent just below – a young girl looked out on it all with cold air in her chest, wondering what would come next for all of them.

And what I need to do to keep them alive.

Rolling a small stone between her finger and thumb, My'ala pressed it against her skin before flicking it away with her nail. She watched it skip over the sand several times, over and over in tiny arcs, before it landed in a small gulley of dust and buried itself, disappearing altogether.

Turning her attention elsewhere, a cold and bitter wind raced over the dune-crest at her back suddenly and tickled down her arms, buffeting her skin in waves. She pulled her cloak tighter about her, hugging her knees to try and conserve some heat – but it seemed no matter how tightly she bound herself, the cool air still seemed to find ways in.

If only I'd brought a blanket—

"You seem rather cold."

My'ala flinched – whether from the gust of cold wind or the sudden voice she wasn't sure – and turned to find Aurelius striding slowly up the dune-side towards her, wearing his informal brown robes. In the low light, the shimmer of his eyes and the brightness of his hair made an eclipsing impression.

"I am rather," she replied with a smile, looking past him to spy no guards following behind. "You've come alone?"

"I've instructed the guards to perform some routine checks with the scouts before people start retiring to their quarters, just as a safety measure," Aurelius explained, settling down next to her and clasping his hands in his lap. "That, and I know they also tend to make you quite… *on edge,* shall we say."

My'ala shrugged, but didn't deny it. "It's quite hard not to feel on edge with them lingering about – although I guess that's the point. They do their job well."

Aurelius smirked. "Yes… although perhaps a little *too* well."

"I guess you could say that." She nodded, looking down at her feet. "What brings you here, anyway? I thought you would've been busy with the others."

"I was… but I thought it was important to come and check up on you, after… well…" Aurelius swallowed, stumbling over himself. "I just wanted to come and make sure you were okay, and ask if you needed anything. What you've been through is no easy thing, and… and I just wanted to check-in, you see."

My'ala heard his words – measured and awkward with so many nuances – and nodded her head slowly. She knew he was trying to bridge a gap by being there, and by offering his words: he was someone born to lead, and raised to be a leader, who now had to overcome emotional technicalities he had never faced before. Feelings he knew, but had never learned to grasp. Sympathy and care; guilt and remorse. Trying to explain a picture with no reference to use. My'ala heard it in his voice and saw it in his pearly eyes.

He cares, she thought, looking out over the camp.

And he doesn't quite know what to do with it.

"I appreciate it, thank you – your words mean a lot, as does your support," My'ala said, watching Aurelius' face relax almost immediately.

"Of course," he replied.

"And while we were travelling, I had a lengthy conversation with Othella about what had happened and *why* it happened, and… I think I've understood a lot of it. I'm still processing, and it takes time… but things are better now. Much better."

The God-Elect smiled. "That is wonderful news, My'ala, I'm... I'm very glad you've found some comfort and peace after it all. As much as I had my initial apprehensions about our newcomer... this Muse appears to be quite an integral part of our journey so far."

"Yes... yes, she does."

In that moment – almost like a spectre in her mind – My'ala sensed Othella's presence somewhere in the camp ahead of her, shifting between the tents. It was like an aura: an energy passing in front of her, illuminating behind her eyes. It bristled over the hairs on her hands and warmed her soul in her chest. She could hardly find the words for it, or the means to understand.

It's like she's ever-present, and always with us...

Our guide, on this long journey forward.

"I'm glad you were able to find some solace with Othella, and could work through some of your feelings," the God-Elect added, drawing My'ala back to the conversation at hand. "I will be the first to admit that she is notably better at it than I am."

"We all have our strengths."

"And I have much to learn."

"That being said," My'ala exclaimed, lifting her finger, "there *was* something I did want to speak to her about, and never got the chance to..."

"Oh? What was it about?"

"It was about a lot of things, really: about the watering hole, and the camp, and what her and I discussed by the reed-beds, and... I've just been pondering a number of things ever since we set out this morning, and I haven't been able to get them off my mind."

The God-Elect acknowledged her with a nod. "Well... I may

not have Othella's nomadic wisdom, but I may be able to help in answering some of those questions. If I may ask, what in particular is troubling you?"

"It's about what we found at the watering hole, and what happened to it… I mean, would it have lasted if we had properly settled? Would the watering hole have fully dried up in the end? Would we have found a way to get by, even if it had? I'm just not sure about any of it, or if we made the right choice…"

Aurelius drew a long breath in through his lips and let it exhale through his nose, looking thoughtfully out on the camp sprawling beneath them. "I've never been sure if there are any true '*answers*' to the choices we make in this life," he said slowly, methodically, "but whatever the case, I can say this much with some certainty: the place we found, and the ideas we had about settling there… they would never have worked in the long run. I don't believe we were ever destined to stay in a place like that, with what we need as people."

My'ala tilted her head, curious about his answer. "What do you mean by that?"

"Well, there just… wasn't enough *there* to make it feel like it could've been something permanent. It lacked some of those key qualities that could make it… you know…"

"…home?"

Aurelius clicked his fingers. "Yes, precisely."

My'ala's eyes lit up.

Perhaps the God-Elect has the answers I seek after all…

"If I may ask," My'ala said, "could you explain what you mean by somewhere having '*the qualities*' to be our home? I've been trying to understand it ever since we left Arbash, and it's proven quite elusive so far."

"Why of course I can," Aurelius replied with a warm, curling smile. Sweeping a hand out, he gestured to the wider camp beneath them, bathed in the warm light of campfires and the fading glow of the sun. "Wherever we go, and whatever we do, we will first seek that which is most necessary to us for our survival. For example, out here on the sands, we search first and foremost for an oasis, because it will provide us with water, and a potential food source from fish. The mud around it is fertile, and may allow us to grow crops. We may find trees, and in turn some natural shelter, or kindling to light our fires. Out here, we seek the things that keep us fed and upright, and allow us to sleep soundly at night. Our basic necessities, if you will."

"Like we do now, when we set up camp."

"Yes! Exactly so. But to talk about what we should be seeking in life, to call somewhere our *home*" – he pressed a hand against his chest – "means so much more to us than just having the means for us to stay alive. The oasis we found, and have since abandoned, offered us those means, it's true. But to form a settlement – and a *society* even more so – we need so much more if it's to last. We need opportunity, and abundance; we need a means to create, and innovate, and grow. We are creatures in motion by our very nature: we need more from life than just our basic survival. Without the room to grow – or the option to do so – we would become restless and depressed: our roots would never take hold, and it would all fall apart from the beginning." The God-Elect took in a deep breath. "For it is the sandstone and mortar that makes a house... but it is the furniture within that makes a home."

Watching him intently as he spoke, with a curiosity she had held since she was a child, My'ala thought back to her house in

Arbash and all the things that reminded her of home. The long dining table under the window that was always bathed in sunlight; the square garden out the back under the shade of bushes and trees; the hibiscus flowers and their elegant spouts, tended to by the tiny hummingbirds that glistened like gold coins.

Analysing it piece by piece, running it through in her mind, it was as Aurelius said: when imagining a place called home, she didn't imagine the safety of the walls or the water that welled up in the sink. She didn't consider the food in the cupboards or the comfort of her bird-feather bed. Such things, although important, hardly crossed her mind when she questioned what home *really* was.

Because instead of that, I think of happy features that bring some joy to my heart, she realised. *Things that I would miss, now they aren't there anymore. Not the things that make the place a house, as such.*

But the things that make a home within me.

Another gust of wind rose up the dune behind her and rippled the robes around her arms; she watched them flutter for a moment like the wings of a bird, and found herself forming a smile.

"So… home can be anywhere, in a way," My'ala explained, "and guides us towards what we should be looking for in this life. Because our necessities are what sustain us… but it's what makes us who we are as *people*, that defines us and our home."

"Now you get it," the God-Elect said, bowing his head. "We need more than just our health, if we're to live happily and peacefully in any one place – and because of that, hopefully you now understand why the oasis we found could never have been our home in the long-run."

"I do understand, yes… it's just a shame that it didn't work out, I guess. We were all so hopeful about it…"

"And we still are, my dear. Just because we've suffered setbacks, doesn't mean we'll persevere any less. We're a strong people, and we look out for each other… and we'll find somewhere, someday soon, that's just right for all of us. I'm sure of it." Aurelius lifted from his seat and brushed his robes down, looking out on the dying sun as its head dipped slowly below the horizon. "What that home looks like, and how many other places we'll have to pass through to get there, I cannot say. But one day we will find that place, and it will feel right in our hearts, and all the struggle we've gone through together will be worth it. With your help – and the guidance of our friend the Muse – we'll make it happen…" – he offered a hand to her, a shimmer in his eyes – "you've just got to keep *looking*."

Gazing up at him – shadowed against the dusky sky of oranges and blues – My'ala took his hand and lifted to her feet, feeling a weightlessness come over her that wasn't there before.

"I shall see you tomorrow, My'ala – I hope you rest well," Aurelius said, running a hand through his hair. "And, thank you for this… it's been nice, and I hope it's helped with some of your concerns going ahead."

"It has, thank you," she replied, acknowledging him with a smile. "I shall see you tomorrow, I'm sure."

"I'm sure."

Laying a hand against his chest, he offered a final bow before turning and descending the slope of the dune, off towards his personal quarters where My'ala spied the pointed helmets of his guards stood waiting.

Turning to the west, she watched the sun edge slowly down

towards the horizon in tiny, incremental shifts. It was beautiful and wonderful, and captivating all in one. It reminded her of hopes and dreams, and starry eyes in ancient sockets. Watching it sinking, slipping slowly out of sight, until the sun's orb gave a final burst of light before it disappeared altogether.

Forming along the horizon in shimmering reams of jade.

IX

FAITH AND PLENTY

What is it?"

"Well… it looks like a mouse, doesn't it? Like that one we had in our pantry a few years ago, back in Arbash. It was a rather cute little creature, now that I remember it… it was almost a shame to see it go."

"It was a shame, and that's mainly because it was just a *normal* little mouse."

"Yes it was."

"But this… *thing,* here… isn't just any mouse, is it, Ma?"

"Whatever do you mean, Mi?"

"Well… this one's got *wings,* to start with."

Walking adjacent to the main convoy of people off to their right, My'ala, her mother and her sister traipsed along the sandbanks like three ancient kings, shrouded in robes as old as time destined for a place unknown. On their backs they bore the components of their tent which they had taken down that morning, distributed evenly between them in neatly-bound cloth sacks. It did add a slight burden to their journey, and the straps often rubbed against their shoulders, but they knew it would allow extra room for the elderly on the carts if they carried it, and that in itself was reason enough to endure any discomfort to come.

Their journey thus-far had been uneventful, with their eyes set firmly on the horizon ahead. The sun beat down against their cowls and the sand ran like water between their toes. Occasional plumes of dust formed with gusts of wind, forcing them to cover their faces and pull cloth gaiters up over their mouths. It did little to deter them, however, as they carried on into the Unknown: a landscape completely devoid of life, for as far as the eye could see.

And then My'ala had spotted something at the top of the ridge next to them: something small and skittish, following them from a safe distance. At first she couldn't make out what it was, against the glaring brightness of the sun. She saw the tiny, snuffling features on its face and assumed it was some kind of rodent; then she saw the membraned wings, and thought in disbelief that it was some kind of bat. The guessing game went on for some time, as her mother and sister got involved too – until one little creature got slightly closer than the rest, daring to venture near them with its face low to the ground, and they realised just how strange the little animals really were.

"It's definitely a rodent of some sort, with a face like that," Su'la deduced, watching one of them bound along the dune-crest with little twitches of its nose. "But its legs are all wrong… the back ones are too large."

"And that's without mentioning the fact it has wings," My'ala added, receiving an eye-roll from her sister.

"Yes, *obviously* with the wings as well. But even that doesn't really narrow down what it actually *is*…"

"What it is, is like nothing I've ever seen before," their mother said with a tinge of disgust. My'ala knew her mother didn't have any particular distaste when it came to the mice they used to find in Arbash – but anything that risked looking like a rat was another matter altogether. "Why do they follow us, anyway? Are they curious, or hungry, or…?"

"It's probably a combination of the two," Su'la replied, adjusting the straps to her bag. "That, and we may be quite close to some underground nest. They probably want to make sure we stay clear of it to avoid it collapsing beneath our feet."

"Hm… how peculiar."

As they spoke, a group of three creatures crested the dune and squabbled amongst themselves briefly, leaping up in great flourishes and flapping their wings with tiny squeaks. The wings extended out from the middle of their spines and appeared to have bones laced within them, so when the sun caught the membranes it looked eerily like a human hand.

"I wonder why they have wings?" My'ala pondered. "I haven't seen anything fly around out here while we've been travelling. Surely the skin just burns in the sun?"

"I don't know about how strong the membranes are, but if I were to hazard a guess I'd say the wings are used to avoid any predators, giving them an extra boost," Su'la explained. "Beyond that, I agree that I don't see much use for them out here."

"What predators would they be escaping, though? We haven't seen any so far," their mother asked in turn, checking the sand at her feet as if something were about to jump out at her.

"It would most likely be snakes I imagine, or some sort of sand worm just below the surface." Su'la smirked, producing a devilish grin. "And although we haven't seen any such creatures so far, probably due to their camouflage… that doesn't mean those same predators haven't seen *you*."

Su'la turned back to the route ahead, pulling the cowl further over her head as My'ala looked down at her feet. She imagined holes opening up all around her suddenly, and the tiny toothy mouths of a hundred sand worms emerging from the earth to hunt. The idea made her squirm, and tense her toes against her sandals – a feeling shared by her mother, so it seemed, by the grimace that crossed her face.

"Do you have to talk about such things?" their mother complained, flinching as she took another step and a section of the sandbank caved in slightly. "We're trying to keep everyone moving… not fearing that their feet will be gnawed off."

"I know, I know… but that's just how nature works," Su'la retorted. "Some creatures survive on what they can find… and other creatures survive by eating those who do the finding."

"And what about us?" My'ala asked. "If we survive on what we find, and eat those who find things too… then what should we be afraid of?"

Su'la produced a measured smile, looking back at My'ala for a moment. "Ourselves, Mi… we have only to fear ourselves."

As her sister turned away again – and their mother shook her head disapprovingly – My'ala jumped at the sound of violent squeaking and the sudden thrashing of sand to her left.

Looking there, she spied the same three mice who had now been joined by a fourth member: one who appeared much larger than the rest, with iridescent black eyes. The other three had worked up into a frenzy at their approach, raising their wings and bouncing on their hind legs in some sort of deterring dance – an act that did little to faze the larger rodent, who regarded My'ala and her family with an obvious discontent.

"They're becoming more numerous," her mother acknowledged.

"And angrier," My'ala added.

"We're probably getting quite close to their nest," Su'la deduced, changing her course slightly. "Best we stay clear of this sandbank for now, so as not to antagonise them anymore."

"I do wonder how they live out here, in such an inhospitable place." My'ala watched the three smaller rodents back down to the larger one, who positioned himself at the crest of the dune and sauntered alongside them. "It can't be easy."

"That's true… but they're resilient little creatures, I'm sure. I imagine they have a good regular way of sourcing food, and an easy place to access—"

Su'la stopped in her tracks, grinding her heels into the dirt so that she almost toppled over.

"What? What is it!" their mother cried, suddenly afraid that something had gone wrong, or some sand worm had come and eaten her foot.

Turning around slowly, Su'la locked eyes with My'ala.

"If they're out here, and can survive as well as they are," she said slowly, "do you think that means that there's—"

"*WATER!*"

A cry, loud and jubilant, tapped through their ears from somewhere ahead of them, near to where the God-Elect's scouts were patrolling.

Their heads all turned to attention, eyes lighting up like tiny fires.

Another cry went up less than a heartbeat later.

"We've found something!"

My'ala felt her heart leap in her chest; Su'la rushed forward and embraced their mother, who whispered a prayer to the skies above and kissed her fingers to her lips.

Looking up the sandbank, the little creatures saw the commotion and scattered, disappearing over the dune-crest into the beyond.

And as they went, My'ala mouthed her thanks, and went on to see what the scouts had found.

First came the green leaves the size of bronze shields, just over the crest of the nearest dune. A dozen or so of them, flapping majestically in the wind like eagle's wings.

Then came their long trunks bristling with tiny brown cones, like the scales of a snake all the way down to some unforeseen roots below.

Then came the sandbank opposite, populated by thorny, tufted bushes, reaching out with branches at jarring angles as if searching the air for moisture. Tiny white flowers and purple-tinged leaves dotted along each thin stem, where even from afar one could see the tiny shapes of flies circling above.

It was new and it was hopeful; it was life, finally, in a place so devoid of it.

And as the people of Arbash took a few more tentative steps forward, they looked down on a land unlike any other, and realised just how lucky they were.

A vast, shimmering lake stretched out beneath them, lined

with tiny springs of mineral-rich water bubbling to the surface in little plumes. The waters were clear and pleasing to the eye; shoals of small-fry and the shadows of larger fish swam about just beneath the surface, topping occasionally to reveal beautiful bellies of soft-silver scales. The outer banks were lined with reed-beds and the circular flotillas of lily-pads, where huge pink flowers the size of baskets soaked up the sun's powerful rays. Dragonflies darted above them, dipping and diving between the tall reeds – keeping their distance from the frogs and lizards that no doubt lurked somewhere below.

Bushes and shrubs dominated the water's edge wherever the reeds did not, sprawling about with dark-green leaves and open hands bearing exotic fruits. There were conical red ones with shells like snake-skin; tiny purple ones that grew together in bunches; round ones the size of a person's hand, with colours that blemished like bruises. They stretched along the branches of spider-like vines and clustered in the undergrowth of heavy-set shrubs.

Everywhere beneath them – cupped in the hands of the desert sands – the fruits of labour blossomed splendidly, guiding the weary travellers forward with its sheer, magnificent bounty.

And at the top of the dune-crest to the west, holding her hands over her mouth in shock, My'ala could not quite believe what they had found, and what it would mean for her people going forward.

"Would you look at that," Othella said alongside her, clasping her hands behind her back with a contented smile on her face. "It's quite a place, wouldn't you say?"

"It's… wonderful," My'ala replied in disbelief. "This isn't some mirage, is it?"

The Muse let out a laugh and smiled even wider. "No, no my dear, this is *very* real, I assure you."

"This is unbelievable. Where's the God-Elect? He must be so relieved by this…"

"From what I understand he's got a head-start on us and is already down there with the others: most likely telling people to exercise caution around these plants and to wait until a proper system is in place. We don't want a repeat of the last place, after all…"

As she said it, My'ala's gaze darted over the thick green bushes and spied Aurelius' beige robes at the outskirts, gesturing openly to the people who had gathered, hoping to get their hands on the first fresh fruits. From what she could make of it, the crowds of citizens seemed to be responding well to his missive, standing by and listening well as Aurelius explained the plan going forward.

"It's good that we're learning from our mistakes," My'ala admitted, "and that the God-Elect is rising to the task at hand."

"That much, my dear, was never in doubt… he's rather tenacious when he wants to be."

"That is very true." My'ala nodded, and let her eyes wander around the bowl of the oasis — setting her sights on a patch of land to the south were the sandbanks seemed to depress slightly. "Is that… actual loose stone there, just beyond the crowds?"

Othella followed her direction, and raised her eyebrows. "I reckon it might just be, you know. It must be from where the oasis has formed and the rock has splintered around the edges."

"We could use it to build with… maybe we could construct an actual *shelter* using some wood from one of those trees." A look of whimsy and joy passed across her pupils. "We could actually start building *homes*…"

Othella held out a hand. "Now wait, let's not get ahead of ourselves… there's still a lot of work to do and a lot of stuff to put in place before we can think about anything permanent. As it stands we don't know anything about this place: about how the plants grow, or if the fruit's edible… or if we can even drink the water here. There's a lot that needs to happen first."

My'ala nodded, understanding. "But… do you think this is it, Othella?"

The Muse looked over to her. "Is what?"

"You know… our place to call home. *The* place, where we can finally settle and prosper." She gestured ahead. "I mean, providing the water's fine and the fruit is edible… we've got all our basic necessities here, and a means to build should we need it. And, if there's a water source here, who knows if there are any others nearby that could be equally bountiful?" She looked deep into the shimmering eye opposite her, and saw a wealth as deep as the Beyond therein. "Could this be what we've been looking for, at long last?"

The Muse took in a long breath and looked out over the trees towards the horizon beyond, where the heat of the sun made it ripple like sea waves as land and sky became one.

"Perhaps it could be, with enough time and hard work… yes, perhaps it could," Othella replied. "The opportunity lies before us, now more so than ever… so who's to say we shouldn't take it in our hands and see what fate has in store for us?"

My'ala smiled broadly, satisfied with her answer, and returned her gaze to the oasis ahead.

Maybe this is finally our place to stay, she thought, listening to the grinding gears of the baggage carts as they trundled over the dune alongside her. *Maybe this is the kind of place where we can grow and prosper, just like Aurelius said.*

Glancing to her right, she watched the carts crest the dune and sag as they tipped down over the other side, their pillared wheels kicking sand up behind them as they burrowed deep into the earth. They were each laden with bags and belongings and the deconstructed parts of various family tents. They were fully stocked, ready to be unloaded as soon as they reached the oasis below – all except one, that was, that passed alongside My'ala last.

A cart with a canopied roof, and the figure of a man tucked away inside.

We made it, da, she thought, allowing a few tears to crease in the corners of her smile. She watched the cart slide gently down the slope all the way to the bottom, and felt her heart lurch after it, almost in fear of letting it go. Imagining him there; imagining his eyes, and his smile.

My'ala lifted a hand, and touched it against her chest.

I can't wait to show you soon.

X

STABILITY

It took most of the day to finally settle and unload the carts at the oasis, occupying the idle hands of every citizen from the old to the whimsically young. At the behest of the God-Elect and his calm coordination, they went about their tasks dutifully with a refreshed sense of purpose that had nearly been lost out on the dunes. Plots of land were demarked with care to avoid encroaching on the luscious green vegetation; small stones were used to prop tent-poles aloft so they did not disturb the soil beneath. The natural springs that formed the watering hole became the only place to gather water, leaving the clay banks around its edge free of human touch. And, after significant assessment by the God-Elect's personal guards, the various fruits and nuts that blossomed in the bushes were deemed safe enough for the people to eat — although access to them was always through an intermediary, to discourage people taking more than their fill.

So as late afternoon set, the camp was finally complete, and the reluctant nomads of Arbash began to settle once more. They were wearied and fatigued from their journey, but still retained their stirrings of hope as they had done before. Gathering their belongings and sharing stories; remarking on the new berries and fruits, and their wonderful tastes on their tongues; taking shelter from the worst of the heat beneath their canopies, with their families and friends close by. As a collective, they took relief as a sense of order returned, surrounded by a natural beauty not unlike the twinkling cove under the archway of Arbash back home. It was a time of peace and reflection, in many ways. A time of respite, with bruised feet and aching bones. And whether the peace was for now or forever, the people of Arbash could not know.

But we should count our blessings all the same, My'ala thought with a smile, *and make the most of this paradise we've found.*

"Mi?"

My'ala blinked and looked across from her, to see her sister sat opposite under the shade of a massive leaf. They had found a quiet patch in the undergrowth to take shelter from the sun's imposing heat, surrounded on all sides by the tall green trunks of strange, overlapping plants. The leaves were a vibrant green and some stretched as wide as sails. Many of them also had tiny fruits nestled in the apex of their fronds, their yellow leaves growing in unique little spirals.

"Is everything alright?" Su'la asked, pushing the huge leaf up to show her face. "You seemed leagues away, then."

"Yea… I was, sorry."

"You know, if you're worried about the God-Elect's guards

finding us, I wouldn't fret too much: I'm pretty sure they've already checked this area, and given it the all-clear."

My'ala winced at the reminder, and looked out between the trunks to her left. *I hadn't been thinking about that... but now I definitely am.* She knew that Aurelius had issued a general decree for people not to venture out into the plants – and had assigned his own two guards the task of checking for any dangers therein – but her sister had convinced her to shirk the rules and sneak into the undergrowth anyway, reimagining adventures they used to have when they were younger that almost always ended up with them in trouble.

Let's just hope this isn't a repeat of that, and we can avoid being discovered out here, My'ala prayed, listening out for the *thud* of footsteps to indicate someone was passing through. *Because although I have a good relationship with Aurelius... I think defying his direct orders may cause quite a big problem.*

For me, and for Su'la.

"It's nice here, don't you think?" her sister mused, looking up through the folds in the leaves to spy the shimmering light of the sun high above. "It's peaceful."

"It is," My'ala conceded, taking a long draw of air. "After being out on the sands for so long, surrounded by other people all day... you almost don't realise just how much you need some quiet space every once in a while."

"It's good for the soul."

"It certainly feels like that."

"And these plants are remarkable." Su'la lifted her hand and ran her fingers along the leaf's flat underside, passing over the ridges that formed its spine. "Who'd have thought somewhere like this could exist in such a barren place..."

"It is rather remarkable..." And My'ala truly meant that as

well. After spending so long in a world of yellows and whites, to be in the thick of green vegetation was very soothing to her soul. It steadied her pulse, and eased the muscles in her legs and feet. Every breath was fresh and inviting, like cold water on the skin. Down in the undergrowth, with only the rustling of leaves to keep her company, every other problem seemed so far away for a moment, and she had never felt a joy quite like it.

A place where I can finally think freely at last, My'ala thought with a smile. *And in such an unexpected place…*

How strange.

"It's a good sign, you know, that we've found a place like this with so much life… a very good sign." Almost to illustrate her point, Su'la pointed to the edge of the small clearing they sat in and spied one of the strange mouse creatures that they had seen out on the sands earlier that day. It wove between the trunks of the plants deftly, stopping for but a brief moment to gaze up at the two newcomers before turning tail and dis-appearing into the shadows beyond. "If life can hold out here… and flourish, even, as it so clearly is… then that means this place has some stability, and the right conditions for things to make their home. A good sign for us, as we intend to do just the same…"

My'ala's ears perked up, not unlike the mouse that they had just spotted darting through the bushes. "What?"

"What?" her sister replied, frowning. "Did I say something wrong?"

"No! No, I…"

"What is it, Mi?"

"I…" My'ala rolled her tongue over her teeth. "You ment-ioned about this place having the '*right conditions*' for things to live here, and how those things are a good sign for us as we seek to do the same, and… well, I was just wondering what you meant by it. If you meant anything in particular by it, that is…"

Su'la gave a knowing smile. "You're worried that we're getting our hopes up for something that may not work again, aren't you?"

My'ala shrugged. "That is part of it, I admit… but it's also just knowing what exactly it is that we should be *looking* for out here. What we should be aiming for. Because this place looks to be a paradise… but I still can't quite put my finger on *why*…"

"It's a very good question," Su'la exclaimed, running a hand through her hair, "and one that can be answered, I believe, not by looking at what is here around us… but by what that *symbolises* to us looking ahead."

"Stability," My'ala inferred.

Her sister nodded and smiled. "Glad to know you do actually listen sometimes!"

My'ala smirked and stuck her tongue out; her sister returned the gesture with a laugh and a grin.

Yea… she's still the same sister alright.

"So, what is it that you want to know in particular?" Su'la asked. "It's quite a broad question, after all."

"I guess the main thing I'm looking for is: what does it mean for somewhere to '*be stable*'? What is that?"

Her sister considered, biting at her lip habitually, before placing her hands flat against the earth at her sides. "Place your hands on the floor for me a moment."

My'ala did so, frowning, feeling the soft, compact dirt against her palms.

"Now, what makes that stable?"

"What, the *dirt*?"

"Yea, the *dirt*."

Furrowing her brow even more, My'ala pressed her fingers into the ground and felt the earth give way slightly – but only a little bit, as she came up against the thick knots of underground roots.

"Well the dirt is, uh… it's compact, not like sand… it's dry… there are uh, roots beneath it… and you can stand on it and it… doesn't slide away?" My'ala tried to explain.

"That's good, that's all true… those *are* things that make the ground stable." Reaching behind her, Su'la next placed her hand around the trunk of one of the strange plants, letting her fingers pull at the fronds of the leaves. "And now this: what makes this plant stable?"

"I mean, it's… it's strong and supportive… it can stand up by itself, and… and it can grow leaves, I guess?"

"Yes, yes… okay… and last but not least" – reaching overhead, Su'la clasped the sides of the massive leaf that sheltered her from the sun – "what about this?"

What is she getting at? "Well it's um… it's clearly well-fed, as it's grown so large, and… it can stand upright and doesn't snap, and… um…"

"Okay, okay, that's good… you get the principle, which is the important thing, so that's always a positive," Su'la said with a smile, turning and assessing the stem of the leaf behind her.

My'ala opened her mouth to speak but found her words confounded by her confusion. "But… I don't understand…" she muttered. "What… *principle* am I meant to be understanding with this? What about——?"

With a tug of her arms, and a great *snap* of vertebrae, Su'la ripped the massive leaf from the plant's tall trunk and placed it down in front of her.

My'ala pressed up on her hands almost instantly, leaning forward with a look of shock on her face. "Whoa, what are you doing!"

"What do you mean?" her sister asked.

"You can't do that!"

"Why can't I?"

"Because… you've damaged it!"

"In the short term, yes, I have." She paused. "And, if I'm honest, I do feel quite bad about it."

"Why did you do it, then?" My'ala challenged, surprised by the hurt in her voice. *It's just a plant…*

"I did it, so that I could ask you a question… about the question you asked me first."

Subtly, slowly, Su'la passed the leaf to My'ala, who took it in her hands like a wreath of flowers and stared at it intently.

"My question to you is, dear sister: is the plant behind me still stable, now that I've removed this leaf?"

My'ala felt the waxy surface of the leaf against her fingertips. "Yes it is, but… less so," she mumbled. "Because you've removed part of its whole."

"So, the plant remains stable, but has been made less so by removing its leaf… and when the wound of the lost leaf heals, and the plant grows a new one back?"

"It will be the same again… as it was before." My'ala looked across to her sister, and blinked. "It'll be stable again, and whole."

"*Exactly* so." Her sister nodded, squinting at the sunlight that filtered down through the other leaves overhead. "Stability, Mi… is *strength sustaining*. It is to face down odds that may be otherwise unassailable, and to prevail against them nonetheless. This plant at my back is strong and has firm roots, and has likely been here a very long time. And even though this plant has suffered setbacks -- when the leaves become damaged, or its seeds don't sow -- the plant lives on regardless, strong and resolute, because it is made to last that way... and so it shall remain forevermore." She gestured out into the undergrowth to their right: out towards the camp, and their people. "We have suffered, and we have endured setbacks on this journey we've undergone... and those setbacks have rocked us, and challenged us, and made us question ourselves in ways we never thought we'd have to. And yet, despite all of that... we are still here, and we still all work together, and we have found a place on firm foundations where we can learn to be a whole again."

Su'la stood up and brushed her legs down before placing her hands on her hips.

"So in answer to your question," she continued, "about what I mean when I say that this place is '*stable*'... I mean that the life here, and what it signifies, is a reflection of what we aspire to be. We have suffered as they have, and we have prevailed as they have. And because of that, we hope to be like the trees and the flowers one day too..." Lifting her hand to the sun, she watched the rays of light fall between her fingers. "Strong, and everlasting... setting roots in a place we can call home."

Looking up at her -- as she had done numerous times in her life, with the same admiration as she felt then -- My'ala rose to her feet and brushed the leaf above her head away, stepping out into the light that seeped through the canopy above. All around her, the leaves rustled and the trunks creaked, and the sun leaking down through the towering fronds above radiated warmly against her face.

It's remarkable, she thought, reaching out and touching the leaves at her sides. *It's all so strong, and defiant. It survives out here against the odds, nurtured by the waters of the oasis. It does not wilt and it does not burn despite the sun's intensity above. It's resilient, and powerful.*

Much like us, in so many ways.

"Thank you for explaining that to me, Su'la," My'ala said softly, brushing her hand against the back of her sister's arm. "I feel I'm beginning to understand what's so special about this place after all."

"It's my pleasure, Mi," Su'la replied, smiling and squeezing her shoulder. "It's a wonderful place, and should be cherished for as long as we have it."

"I can't wait to explore it more in the future."

"Neither can I, it's true – but all in due time, as I'm sure you know." She tapped the side of her nose. "Besides, it's getting on and we best be getting back soon. We can't have people start asking questions about where we've been and what we've been up to—"

"*Hello!*"

My'ala's heart stalled in her chest and a gasp escaped her lips; opposite her, Su'la's eyes went wide like too glistening sea pearls.

Somewhere on their right, a faint rustling caught in their ears.

"*Is there anyone out there! We told you kids to stay out of this place!*"

"It's the guards!" Su'la whispered loudly, grinning like a little girl as she looked over her shoulder.

"I thought you said they'd already checked this place!"

"Apparently not—"

"*We'll find you!*"

Su'la grabbed My'ala by the shoulder. "Quick, run, *run!*"

Wasting no time, My'ala turned tail and scampered off through the undergrowth, swatting away spindly vines and impressive sail-like leaves. She followed the yellow-brown dress of her sister, who charged through the greenery as they picked up the pace — like they had done when they were children, running from trouble in the hopes they wouldn't get caught.

Up ahead, Su'la laughed, opening her arms out wide.

Just like old times, My'ala thought with a grin, giggling to herself as they ran.

XI

THE MIRAGE

Walk with me, will you?"

Dusk had fallen, and the sky was an ashen colour like a cave painting on stone. Threads of waning orange intertwined with strands of purple, as the tired sun slipped over the horizon and beckoned the night sky forth. There were trails of thin clouds in the sky overhead, forming in a myriad of colours like fish oil on water. Stars twinkled beyond them, flashing and rippling in waves.

And above it all, the impossibly vast Beyond yawned and stretched in slumber, covering the world expanse of the night sky for as far as the eye could see.

And yet, despite the encroaching twilight, the people of Arbash were just as active as they had been in the day, full of joy and merriment at the sanctum they had found. Their fires bellowed brightly as people sang and danced together, sampling the new fruits they had discovered with gleeful, juice-coated smiles. Children chased each other down torchlit paths, giggling and screaming all the way. Some families had even opened out blankets to lie and gaze up at the stars, recounting memories and admiring the constellations that glistened in the darkness high above.

A change had come over the nomads, after their long journey over the sands: whatever weariness they had possessed on their arrival had almost completely gone. In its place, an overwhelming joy had arisen that swept their exhaustion away, marvelling at the bounty they had found and the prayers that had been answered.

And as she walked amongst them – waving to people who had seemed so glum the previous day, and raising glasses to those who she thought had lost hope – My'ala found her relief was so strong that it nearly knocked her from her feet. Seeing their happiness was contagious; watching the belief rekindle in their eyes was nearly enough to bring tears to her own.

It's beautiful to see, My'ala thought, smiling at another family roasting food over their fire. *It's validation of our struggles so far, and what we've sacrificed to get here. We may have found an answer to all of our collective dreams.* She paused. *Now we can only hope it lasts this time.*

For all of our sakes.

"Would you like a berry?" Othella asked at her side, plucking at a vine of small, pink-coloured fruits. They were strange looking in the low light, with their skin covered in tiny indents like the pores on someone's skin – but clearly their unappealing texture was little more than a ruse, as Othella took great joy in biting through another.

"I… yea, sure." Reluctantly, My'ala reached over and plucked one from the vine, rolling it between her fingers and bristling at the odd shape. "Thank you," she said, holding it up at eye level. "And may I ask, what is it, exactly?"

"It's one of the new fruits that the God-Elect has deemed safe for us to consume… as much as it doesn't look like something that should be edible." Othella took another bite out of hers, using her front teeth to carve it open like a mouse. "They're calling it a… *lie-chee*… I think? It has some meaning in an old language that I profess I don't really understand, but either way it tastes rather nice…"

My'ala gave the small fruit another calculated glare, trying to work out what it would taste like, before she popped the whole thing in her mouth and bit down—

"Oh no, you don't want to—"

My'ala felt a seismic *crunch* against her back teeth suddenly and cursed under her breath, spitting the tiny fruit out onto the sand at her feet. Studying the remnants with a look of disgust, she spied the culprit amongst the remains of the fruit: a tiny pit like a shiny round stone wedged in the dirt.

Lifting a hand, My'ala pressed a finger against her molars, and looked over to the Muse with a raised brow. "You didn't think… to tell me about that… *before* I took a mouthful?"

"In fairness, I didn't think you were going to eat the whole thing in one go." She smirked. "You once again prove just as unexpected as ever…"

My'ala rolled her eyes and grunted.

"Did you get a chance to sample it, though? How did it taste?"

"I can't say I had it… in my mouth… long enough to get a decent taste." My'ala pulled her finger out of her mouth and was relieved to find no blood. "Next time I try one – and don't *break* my *jaw* in the process – I'll let you know what I think."

Othella nudged her arm. "That's the spirit."

"Why did you want to walk with me, anyway?" My'ala inquired, looking to the path ahead. "I hope it wasn't just to try and break my teeth on unusual fruits…"

Othella smiled. "No, nothing as devious as that, I assure you," she replied. "I just wanted to catch-up and see what you make of our new settlement, and how things are going. A lot has happened so far, after all… as our dear friend the God-Elect knows all too well…"

The Muse gestured ahead of them, and My'ala followed her direction to spy a gathering of people huddled together under torch-light, pulling their robes tight across their bodies to keep out the worst of the night cold. There were people of all ages there, from the elderly propped up on walking canes to young children clinging to the legs of their parents.

And, stood above them all on a wedge of stone on the far side, My'ala spied the red-and-white garb of Aurelius, expressing openly with his hands. He appeared to be in the middle of an address of some sort, speaking with an air of authority with his guards flanking him to either side.

Approaching the rear of the crowds, Othella suggested that they listened in on what Aurelius had to say – and, without much choice, My'ala did just that, picking apart the disparate noises to find Aurelius' voice.

"…and so our prayers have been answered at last, and now we stand in a place of true abundance that we can all enjoy together," he said to the nods and agreement of the crowd. They were captivated by his every word, as if he'd cast some ancient spell. "Here we stand on the precipice of greatness, ready to step into our new lives as we step away from our time as nomads, true to the knowledge that we have endured great hardship… and that what we have found we ultimately deserve…"

"*He speaks well,*" the Muse whispered.

"*He means it, too,*" My'ala replied.

"*Let's see where it goes…*"

"But now that we're here… and now that we've settled… some of you may be asking questions about what this place means to us, and what we should do going forward," Aurelius continued, placing a hand on his chest. "It is true that we have faced many setbacks in coming to this place. We have struggled, and we have rationed, and we have marched out into the Unknown for many long days and nights. And in that time, we found a place that we believed could have been our home… but due to our *overzealousness* in finding fresh water, we took from the land more than it could give… and were forced to move on once more. It is a fact that I know has weighed on your minds for quite some time now, and in arriving to this place you may have fears that a similar fate will befall us again."

A few nods passed through the crowds; parents stroked their children's hair comfortingly.

"But I want to assure you, here and now, that we will not be ravaged by the same problems that drove us from the last place we found… and that is because this land before us will bring new challenges of its *own*, that we must face together if we hope to come out of this *alive*." The God-Elect's face was stony and resolute; a few frightened murmurs passed through the crowds. "To say this land will bring us nothing but fortune, is to invite serpents into our homes. To say that this place will satisfy us fully, is to invite ungratefulness into our hearts. We cannot know what lies ahead of us on our quest to make this our home… and we cannot shy away from the challenges that will arise when trying to make that a reality."

"*I don't understand,*" My'ala whispered, feeling her stomach turn. "*Shouldn't this be more… positive? We've found a beautiful haven, full of riches…*"

"*Perhaps in time we will rejoice…*" Othella replied, inclining her head towards the crowd. "*But when so many things can still go wrong, true relief will always allude us…*"

"So, I say to you all, gathered here now: take joy in this new paradise that we have found, and remind yourself of the hope you carried with you from the gates of Arbash to get here," Aurelius proclaimed. "But do so always with caution, both for yourselves and your neighbours. We must take stock of our supplies, and enforce quotas on our water; we must keep the soil beneath our feet intact so the plants may continue to grow. We have happened upon this beautiful place by chance, so let us not forget just how precious that is…" He paused forebodingly. "And how easily it can all fall away if we aren't careful…"

Lifting his hand, the God-Elect cradled his fingers against the starlit sky, whispering a quiet prayer under his breath before bowing to the crowds below. They were already beginning to disperse, shuffling back to their communal tents with sombre, determined looks, weighing up the God-Elect's words and what it meant for them going forward. Aurelius watched them all go, slipping into the night one by one until the circle of torch-light was completely cleared. Even then he lingered for a while, grinding his teeth together in his mouth, before My'ala saw him release a tired sigh and step off the platform beyond.

"He looks distressed," My'ala muttered, a lingering pain in

her heart.

"I imagine he is, considering the circumstances," Othella replied, drawing her robes tighter. "I would be in his place."

"But why? We're safe here."

"Safety is only part of it."

"And this place has everything we need… *more* than we need, even!"

The Muse produced an awkward smile. "Yes… it does."

My'ala furrowed her brow. "Is that… *not* a good thing?"

Othella sighed, looking up to the deep, dusky sky at the horizon. The oranges had all but disappeared, bleeding out into blues and purples like the far reaches of the sea. Her eye glistened as she looked on, reflecting a world of mystery – My'ala studied it intently, a thousand questions coiling about in her head.

"Othella, are—"

"I lived in a paradise once, long ago… in a place far from here that many could hardly believe existed," the Muse interrupted, not taking her eyes off the horizon. "A massive city – tenfold larger than the one you called home – that had grown from the heart of a single spring bubbling up endlessly from the sands. It was a place of walls and palaces and citadels. It was a place of grandeur and abundance, housing many thousands of people. A place of riches and wonders, far beyond what you have ever known…"

"Another *city*… out *here?*" My'ala said in disbelief, looking off into the distance to imagine huge spires and walls suddenly emerging from the dunes. "How? I didn't think it was possible…"

"Under the right conditions, with enough good luck and judgement, anything is possible out here my dear… anything at all."

"But… if this place was so grand and magnificent… then why did you leave? Why venture out into the harshness of the desert when you had everything you could ever want?"

"Because despite its grandeur and abundance… there was also something very wrong right at the city's heart, rotting it from the inside like an overwatered flower. Wilting its petals; turning it away from the sun. Weakening its stem, so the whole thing began to fall…"

"What was it?"

Othella pursed her lips, a dark shadow crossing her eye. "It was *greed*, my dear… that which befalls those who have everything, but still want so much more." She ran her fingers along the hem of her robes, tracing the silver knots there.

"*Greed…*" My'ala mouthed, recalling conversations she had had with her father back in Arbash, and the twisting pain the memory brought in her chest as the serpent rattled its tail. She thought of the toolmakers and the farming engineers, and her father's hard decisions just to put food on their table. All of the empty lots around his workhouse, and the people who had once occupied them.

Glancing over to Othella then – her single eye still fixed to the horizon beyond – My'ala saw a lot of her father's face reflected there all of a sudden: a mixture of stoniness and guilt, addled with remorse and the toll of hard choices.

A face that has suffered at the hands of others… and has survived with the scars to prove it.

My'ala swallowed painfully. "What happened to you?" she asked.

"I was a merchant, for a time… working in the local markets, trading exotic spices that our scouts found in the desert," the Muse explained, her voice noticeably level. "We were part of a guild – a group of fellow spice merchants, all collaborating together – and things were looking up for us for a while. We were making good profits, and got on well with our rulers... money was good, and we did well." She released a sigh, exhuming the full weight of her chest. "And then, one day... one of my competitors grew rather restless, and decided to seize the competition for himself..."

She lifted a hand to her face, and slid a finger under her damaged eye. "A group of masked figures came into our warehouse one night, armed with sharp knives and nasty blades, and attacked us while we worked. We had no-one there to protect us, and the nearest barracks were several blocks away. We managed to fend them off for a while, it's true, losing a number of our own in the process... but not before they sent my warehouse up in flames, and took from me one thing I could never get back..."

My'ala listened intently, and nodded, and studied the lines around Othella's ruined eye in the failing light of dusk. There were scars there, she knew, and not just ones visible to her: scars of betrayal and sadness, and the results of falling victim to someone's personal greed. There were the scars of things she had lost, and discovered through that loss. Losing everything she had known in a single night...

And surviving long enough to tell the tale.

"I've made my mistakes, in life, I know... and you may argue that I've paid the price for them, too," Othella continued, turning to face My'ala at last. "I've worked, and I've suffered, and I've carried on regardless with my morals still intact... but on that journey I've also learned a thing or two, about what people are, and what they should look for in life. That doesn't mean I have all the answers – I wouldn't have posited such a big question to you when we first met if I did – but it does mean I know a couple of things for certain, and one of them is this…" Their eyes locked, and the Muse's face became statue-like and dark. "You can have everything in life… everything and more, even… and to some people that will be enough, and they will house in their hearts nothing but gratefulness for it. But there will also be some, despite the abundance they face, who still aren't satisfied with that… and it's only a matter of time before they start looking for something more… until *greed* is all they find…"

Off to the side of them, a flash of green light flickered across their eyes as the sun dipped below the horizon.

Reaching out, Othella placed a hand on My'ala's shoulder and squeezed it tight, never quite managing a smile.

"Now I must go, and… be alone for some time," the Muse said softly, turning away and pulling the cowl over her head. "I wish you well, my dear… get some sleep, and think on what I've said. And please, take joy in what we've found, and the hope it brings… you've all worked hard for this, and deserve more than anything some time to rejoice. But as the God-Elect said, always be vigilant… because a blessing and a curse will always go hand in hand."

Turning from her like a ghost conjured from a storm, Othella slipped away into the night, her green robes morphing with the gloomy sands until she disappeared from view altogether.

Leaving My'ala alone in the dark.

Imagining something like home.

XII

PARADISE

Five days later...

Good morning, da, it's... it's good to see you again."
Tentatively, she reached over and brushed his hand, feeling his cool skin against her knuckles in the shade of the canopied cart.

"Your breathing sounds better, and... and there's more colour in your face, too, you'll be glad to hear. You don't look so pale anymore, which I know has always been a concern of yours!" She smiled fleetingly, then sighed. "I'm... sorry I didn't come to see you yesterday: I know I try and make an effort to see you every day, but everything just got really busy and I wasn't sure how long things would take and time ran away from me and... I guess it just slipped my mind. Not *you*, though... you didn't slip my... I hope you don't think you slip my mind, da, because you never do, and I…" She clenched and unclenched her hands, swallowing painfully. "Things are going well here, you should know… they're going really well, in fact. Everyone's getting on well and working together. The tents are staying up, and the water hasn't dried up, and the bushes remain abundant with food. We haven't encroached on it at all, and have even managed to set down a few foundations for future buildings. I know that sounds quite premature but… you know how things like that give hope to people, and… well, we could all do with a bit more of that at times, you know, and…" She lifted a hand to her face and wiped her eyes. "I just wish you could see it, da… it's amazing, and important, and it makes us all believe again. I wish you could see it… it'd make you smile – or maybe not smile, but, you know, not look *as* grumpy as usual… or, um…"

She reached forward and touched the cloth sacks at his feet, gritting her teeth together to stop the emotion overwhelming her.

"Just come back to us soon, okay? Just come back to us and… and tell us it's okay. I know you were never big on words, but… we need you right about now, wherever you are…" Her face creased up, knotting with tears. "I just miss you so *much*… I miss you, and I can't wait to show you what we've done here, together. Just, please come back, da… please…"

She took a single step back and let her hand slip from the edge of the cart, the tiny echoes of memory spilling from her fingertips as she left his side once again. Placing two fingers to her lips, she kissed them and touched them against her chest, imagining his bright face as he awoke and saw the home that they were trying to create. Imagining his soft smile as he saw his wife and daughters again, and held them close in an embrace that went on forever. Admiring the beautiful waters and green plants of the oasis; admiring the people working together for a greater good, creating new livelihoods of stability and hope. The sudden joy in his face, as he took his first deep breath, and concluded among many things that life would be okay.

The only words I need to hear, My'ala thought. *More so now than ever.*

Turning from the cart, she paced back out into the desert on shaky, unbalanced feet. Ahead of her, her sister and mother stood waiting, shadowed by one of the God-Elect's guards who had their head bowed in respect. As promised, the guards had been caring for her father day-in and day-out, dutifully giving him water and adjusting his limbs to keep his body working. Their tireless work had been what had kept him alive since his collapse over a week before.

And may the gods bless them for it, My'ala added, *and return him to us one day.*

"How is he, Mi-Mi?" her mother asked, leaning forward to hold her shoulder and run a hand through her hair. "How are you?"

"I'm fine, ma… and da's fine too," she replied, squeezing her hand. "He's keeping well, and has a lot more colour in his face than when I last saw him."

"Oh, that's good! That's… good…" Her mother reached out again almost instinctively to cradle My'ala's face, but pulled her hand away and gave a warm smile instead. She had become more physically affectionate with them both since their father had fallen ill and developed his horrendous cough. It was some form of comfort to her, to show her love more in the face of uncertainty, and with her own mental fragility to take into account her daughters were likely the only thing that kept her going.

And we're happy to be, no matter what, My'ala thought, smiling back at her ma. *We're in this together, after all.*

No-one's left behind.

"The guards have some good news about da's condition, too," Su'la said, looking as stoic and resolute as she always seemed to. "They say that, with his current rate of improvement, he may start waking up in the next few days, and he could even open his eyes, too!"

"That's… incredible to hear," My'ala replied softly, looking over to the guard stood adjacent to them. "And I just want to say thank you to you and your colleague for your work and diligence in helping our father… it's because of you that he is so near to returning to us, and we couldn't be more grateful."

"I am simply doing my duties, miss," the guard said, bowing their head to her. "Every soul deserves a chance, and every family deserves a father."

"Thank you so much." She glanced back to the cart for a brief moment. "I can't wait to show him what we've started to create here…"

"I think what you mean, is what *you've* started to create here, Mi-Mi," her mother corrected, sweeping a hand across to the oasis beyond. "It's thanks to your hard work and kindness that we have so much to look forward to here… you should know that. And know that *he* will be very proud of it, too."

"I hope so." She nodded, and smiled at her mother. *I really do.* "And that reminds me, I have a few things that I've agreed to do this morning, so would I be okay to excuse myself and, you know…"

"By all means, Mi," Su'la replied with a look of pride. "Go

do your thing."

"We'll be back at camp if you need us," her mother added, hesitant but understanding. "Don't stress yourself out too much, will you?"

"I'll try not to." She brushed her robes down and looked out across the oasis to the north. "Besides, I have the God-Elect to help me out with trying to keep this all together. Knowing what he's like, I'm sure he's got everything under control…"

"It's out of control," Aurelius grumbled under the shade of a mobile canopy, pinching the bridge of his nose with his fingertips. A small cloud of buzzing insects had joined him under the cloth cover, which he seemed to swat at with his hand almost continuously in an attempt to divert them elsewhere. So far, his efforts had failed – and it did little to improve his mood, at that. "I'm trying to think of a reason for why they would do it… but even that seems to be alluding me at the moment." He looked off towards the mass of tents with a scowl. "Why would they *take* what isn't *theirs?*"

On the eastern side of the oasis – where the green vegetation gave way to gnarled old bushes spotted with tiny white flowers – the God-Elect stood on a lonesome sandbank with one of his personal guards, surveying the landscape beyond and the citizens that shuffled across it. From his vantage, he could see across the entire span of their encampment, like a vulture soaring over the dunes in search of a fresh meal. Following the paths of people and noting the bags they carried; assessing every turn of the head or gesture of the hands. Making mental notes and forming plans, with his claws twitching hungrily in the hope of catching his prize. And although My'ala knew the God-Elect's intentions were nowhere near as morbid as a vulture's, the grey shadows around his eyes and the stern glare he gave their camp in that moment could have quite easily suggested otherwise.

"What's been happening?" My'ala asked cautiously, wiping beads of sweat from her forehead. "Is it the thieves again, stealing the berries?"

"Yes... although there have been some developments on that front since we last spoke," Aurelius replied, his lips little more than a thin line. "None of them good, I might add."

"What are they?"

"Well, despite our best efforts, the thieves have remained a constant problem for us in the green spaces... where we're still trying to limit access so as not to disturb the plant-life there."

"A smart move."

"Yes... but the thieves in question monitor our nightly patrols, then sneak past when no-one's looking, and make off with bunches of these small red berries that we've seen growing along some of the vines there."

"What do they do with the berries, and why do they want so many of them?"

"Well, this is the issue: as far as we've seen, there's nothing interesting or different about them *at all*. They are, in nearly every way, exactly the same as any other fruit we've found in the green areas so far." He paused. "Or that was... until this morning, when we followed their tracks from last night... and believe we've finally worked out what the berries are being used for."

With a grimace, Aurelius gestured to the luscious green leaves and blossoming branches next to them.

"We found a cluster of the berries, which had evidently been dropped by the thieves, in one of the small openings that appear within the deeper parts of the vegetation," he explained. "At first we took no notice of it, as the berries had started to go off and had flies around them… but then a *smell* hit us, like nothing we've ever smelt before… and my guards and the volunteers who were helping us, they started to feel quite faint and dizzy, and started laughing at each other in strange ways. It was like the smell had turned them delirious, or something."

"How odd," My'ala said, looking puzzled. "Did they taste any of the berries to see if it definitely was them?"

"We did not… although you would be hard pressed to convince me they were *not* the cause of the strange smell. It was so pungent, and with the flies being drawn to it as well… it just had to be them."

"And what does that mean for the thieves who've been taking them? Do you think they're hoping to use the berries to make more of this… *stuff* that you found?"

"It's the best theory we have at the moment, yes," Aurelius confirmed, then sighed. "Although what they intend to do with it, and how they intend to use it, has completely alluded us. They come and go in the night like foxes… and we're left none the wiser come morning."

My'ala nodded, and looked out over the mass of tents to their left, spying there dozens of different faces going about their daily routines. There was nothing unusual about the scene she was presented with: nothing to suggest there was trouble afoot, or that people were becoming rebellious. They all appeared as unassuming as ever, with the chance of identifying any one particular thief practically next to none.

Because they're all good people, My'ala believed – although her understanding of what that meant had been rattled by the news of the thieves. *They're good people, with a few misguided souls amongst them. Every group as an outlier, or someone who defies certain norms.*

But what would then drive them to go and steal, especially against someone's direct orders?

She scanned along the edge of the vegetation, spying a number of different people there: children plucking at the grasses with absent, awkward fingers; men and women stood admiring the colourful flowers; a few other industrious types looking at the tall green stems, no doubt debating what they could be fashioned into once the cordon was eased.

No-one is out of place... no-one is out of sorts. Everyone has exactly what they need, when they need it. My'ala sensed the serpent hiss in her stomach, and squirmed.

Unless that's exactly the problem: that they know they have whatever they could want.

But now they're driven to want more...

"It's a shame really," Aurelius spoke up suddenly, swatting at the flies above his head, "because if people are stealing from those in need and defying my requests in doing so, then a firmer hand will be needed. It's not something I want to do, or take great pleasure in admitting... but if I need to search every alcove of every tent, and scour the green in search of some hidden stash... then I will do so, without a moment of doubt, if people aren't willing to do what's best and admit to their personal crimes. Because at the end of the day, these thieves are acting in their own interests, and are doing so selfishly." He shook his head, his breath rasping. "If you ask me... their actions are nothing short of—"

"*Greedy,*" My'ala whispered. The serpent rattled its tail.

"Yes, exactly so… greedy."

"Yes, I…" The words dried up in her mouth, replaced instead by a newfound urgency that raced with her beating heart. "May I… could I be excused… please?"

Aurelius turned to her – for the first time during their entire conversation – and frowned, his eyes like tiny pinpricks. "Yes, of course… is everything alright? Are you… okay?"

"Yea, I… I just need to go and see someone, that's all. To clarify something."

"Then by all means, My'ala, I won't keep you… but please do look after yourself." He levelled his gaze with her, shadowed harshly against the sun. "Because I'm not sure if it's the light or not, but…"

"…you look awfully pale, my dear."

Under the shade of one of the tall, ridged trees at the north-eastern edge of the oasis – with a number of strange seeds on the ground that looked almost like spearheads – My'ala lifted a hand to her face and touched the skin on her cheek. It felt gritty beneath her fingertips, lined with dust and sand, and there was a coldness that bristled against the tiny hairs along her jaw. The sensations were not unusual, and didn't indicate she was unwell, but something about the racing of her heart and the angry serpent in her stomach provided other signs that something wasn't quite right.

And I don't know what to do.

"Whatever is the matter?" Othella asked, adjusting the gem-stones of her necklace with a jangle of chains. "You look like you've seen an omen."

"I don't know what's going on, if I'm honest," My'ala admitted, her shoulders slouching. "I'm just so... *on edge*, all of a sudden. I have been all morning."

"Well, whatever for? Is something on your mind?"

"Yea there is, but I... I don't really know how to say it. I just hope we're doing the right thing out here, with all of this, and... I hope that things don't go *wrong*... because I'm worried that they will go *wrong*, and that we aren't doing *enough* to keep everything *right*..." She sighed and rubbed her eyes. "I don't even know what's going on with me..."

"You're concerned, that's all! And why wouldn't you be? Sure, you've had a few problems over the past few days that have set you and the others on edge... but that's only natural, when trying to maintain the good thing that you've created. People are happy; people are *living* again, like they used to back where you came from. That's reason to celebrate, I would have thought..."

"It is, it is, but... I just want that to *continue*. And not just for a little while, but... *forever*. I want these people to feel like they've found a home, and not just a place along the way."

Othella smiled knowingly. "My dear... they *do* think this place is home: I can see it in their eyes, and their smiles. They go about their duties with pride, and are growing together as a community – especially now that they have something solid beneath their feet. And you may come across some people who haven't quite settled yet, it's true... but some people take longer to adjust to these things. Some manage change well... and others, not so much."

"I just want to ease their burden."

"And you're very noble for it, My'ala."

"But will it be enough?" she asked, shivering at a sudden gust of wind. "If bad things do happen… and things do go wrong… will what we have here be enough to survive it?"

The Muse – clasping her hands before her as if in prayer – nodded slowly and drew in a long breath through her nose. Her singular eye seemed to shine very brightly in that moment, elucidating fields of stars.

"No-one can know the answer to that, my dear… not even I," Othella said. "We hope every good thing lasts forever… and we hope that what we've found in life is what we've been looking for all along. But sometimes it isn't, and whether that's within our control or not doesn't really matter." She lifted a finger. "The point is, that we *try*, and we give everything we can to what we cherish. This place that you've started building… the people's lives that you've given hope to… shouldn't be guided on the fear that it will all go wrong one day. Because it *might* all go wrong one day… but when it does, you don't want to languish on the warnings you never saw coming or the instincts you never listened to. You want to embrace what you *have* created, and what *has* gone right… even in the face of it all going wrong." Extended an arm, she pointed in the direction of the camp at My'ala's back. "You've brought these people together with open arms, and given them an opportunity they may never experience again… and that's something to cherish, and work hard for every day. Because these people see you as a leader, and as a force to be reckoned with… but more than that, they see you as the embodiment of the one thing they can't live without…"

Othella tilted her head, and a glint crossed her eye like a shooting star.

"*Hope.*"

My'ala – under the shade of the tree with dragonflies buzzing overhead – released a long breath and smiled with tears in her eyes, letting the air pass through her lips in a delicate, thin stream. She bowed her head, not possessing the words to give a response – watching Othella do the same, her smile growing warm and vibrant.

"Take stead in what you've created, and the hope you bring to these people," the Muse said softly, curling an arm around her shoulder and turning to face the oasis beyond. "Because whatever happens… and whatever goes wrong… the answer to what you should be looking for in life will always be there when you need it…"

Looking out on the dazzling surface of the still, clear water, My'ala sensed her pulse slow in her chest and her hands relax at her sides. She let go of what had been unsettling her, feeling it drift away and spill out over the sand, clearing space in her mind like blue skies after a storm.

But even so, the snake in her stomach continued to rattle its tail, reminding her of memories she hoped to banish.

And a fear that never quite slipped away.

XIII

GREED

At her family's campfire that night, surrounded by an all-consuming darkness, My'ala stoked the loose kindling beneath the flames and let sparks flash across the sand. The red-orange glow of the main fire was oddly mesmerising to her, and she marvelled at how the flames seemed to clash with each other like twisting, sparring swords. It reminded her of her father's fascination with fires, in a way, and his delicate attention to them when they had made camp over the previous weeks. At first she hadn't fully understood why he'd taken such care over it, or why he was so enamoured by the flames – but in that moment, watching the fire shine in her sister and mother's eyes, My'ala felt that she was beginning to understand it at last.

He always had a lovely way of seeing the world.

"Good work with the fire, Mi-Mi," her mother commented, twisting her skewer in the flames. "You're a natural."

"Anyone would think you've got some magic in you with how bright you can get it," Su'la added, winking.

"All the better to cook with," My'ala replied, lifting her skewer to her mouth and taking a bite out of her food. "And this fish is delicious."

"The God-Elect was kind enough to give us one of the larger fish from the oasis on this week's rations, so thought I should make the most of it," their mother said with a smile. "I was worried the fish wouldn't be any good, so I'm glad it's turned out okay…"

"It's more than okay, ma," Su'la said, taking her own mouthful. "It's… delightful…"

"Yes it's very good, thank you ma," My'ala added. Opposite her, over the licking flames, her mother's eyes shone with a warm, emotive glow.

"Speaking of which…" her sister exclaimed, wiping grease from her mouth, "have any of you tried those little lumpy berries they've found? The pink ones?"

My'ala lifted her hand enthusiastically. "I have, yes!"

Meanwhile, their mother frowned. "I can't say I have, no… what berries are these?"

Su'la placed her skewer down and used her fingers to convey the size. "They're about this big, and they're a red-pink colour… and they're covered in these funny little bumps and dips just like a seashell. They're very strange I'll admit, but I can't for the life of me remember what they're called…"

"A *lie-chee,* I think it is," My'ala explained. "Or at least, that's what Othella told me."

"Yea, that sounds about right from what I recall."

Their mother looked between them both and nodded. "How peculiar… and what do these berries taste like, exactly? Are they definitely safe to eat?"

"Yes, ma, we promise you they're safe to eat," My'ala said, exchanging a smirk with her sister. "Although, with that being said, you do have to go careful with the centres of them… as I found out quite suddenly this morning…"

"Oh *please* don't tell me you popped it in your mouth in one!" Su'la said with a chuckle.

My'ala blushed red and ran a hand through her hair. "I might've done…"

"Oh Mi-Mi!" her mother exclaimed, as her sister burst out laughing and My'ala turned even more red. Lifting from her seat, Su'la walked over to her and wrapped her arms around her shoulders.

"I do love you, Mi – bless your soul."

"I love you too, Su'la," My'ala replied, squeezing her hands as her sister let go and stood to one side.

"We'll have to get you one to try at some point, ma," Su'la suggested, "so you can see what all the fuss is about. They're quite nice once you get used to them…"

"We could probably source some in the next lot of rations if we ask," My'ala added.

Their mother scratched her hair reluctantly. "Well, I'm sure I can give it a go… why not, after all!"

She placed her skewer down by her side, the fish-meat on it only half eaten, and looked across the roaring fire at her daughters for a moment. A smile graced her lips, broad and proud: the kind of joyous look that was only possible between a mother and child. Symbolising a bond, everlasting, playing out between them like musical strings, balancing a tune that filled their hearts.

The moment seemed to stretch on forever, the three of them regarding each other with golden light shining in their eyes…

…until their mother spied something in the space behind them, in the gloom of the night beyond, and her brown creased suddenly into a frown.

"Girls…" she mouthed, lifting from her seat.

"Yes?" they replied, opening their hands.

"Where are all of those people going…?"

Turning sharply on her heel – mirroring her sister next to her – My'ala looked out into the clear night air and traced the outskirts of the oasis. There, she spotted a few small groups of people running along the watery banks, towards some unknown destination at the western edge of their camp. They were all wearing light robes and shouting amongst themselves, slipping in and out of firelight as they passed the suspended torches. Stood upwind from them, My'ala couldn't make out what they were saying exactly as they passed – but one word rang out beneath it all nonetheless, striking her like a lightning bolt as soon as it reached her ears.

"*Trouble…*" she mouthed, forgetting to breathe.

Oh no…

Without thinking, she stepped out from under the canopy of their tent and started running across the sands, her sister crying out and taking off in pursuit behind her.

My'ala had no recollection of her surroundings as she hurtled forwards, driving her legs down into the compact sand, gliding past the guide-lines of the tents that shimmered like silk in the moonlight.

There were voices behind her, and all around her. Her heart thumped in her head. Sweat beaded over her skin despite the biting cold of the night air.

Still she ran on, charging between the tents, in and out of the shadows like a spirit, watching people flock alongside her towards whatever was causing the commotion—

When she stumbled suddenly, losing her footing on a stray stone that skittered off over the dirt—

Her hands lurched out, ready to catch her if she toppled, but she managed to plant her feet down again just in time, grinding to a halt as the sand rose up her ankles in waves—

She swayed for a moment, blinking heavily, trying to catch her breath again as the shock racked her system.

Behind her, her sister appeared and wrapped her arms around My'ala's waist, her breath rasping through her nose in panicked spurts.

"Mi, for grief's sake, you can't just run off like… like…"

Su'la's mouth fell shut like a trapdoor, leaving the statement unfinished. Looking ahead, she let go of My'ala and stepped forward, curiosity and fear marring her expression.

"Mi… what in the Beyond is going *on*…?"

Ahead of them both – between the last of the tents marking the eastern edge of their camp –the rocky outcrop where Aurelius gave his speeches stood loftily in the dark, the empty circle before it surrounded by tall, burning torch-poles.

Except, for whatever reason, the torchlit circle was far from empty that night: because everywhere My'ala looked, she spied people huddled in robes, staring off at something to their left that remained just out of sight..

"Look, there! The God-Elect is talking to some people," Su'la said, pointing off to the far side of the torchlit circle. "And it doesn't look good, whatever it is…"

My'ala took a single step to the right, expanding her view of the scene beyond, and there she saw Aurelius and his personal guards bathed in orange light, positioning themselves at the head of the crowds just as Su'la had said. All three of them were clearly very agitated, as the God-Elect gestured broadly between himself and the gathering citizens, trying to get a point across that clearly wasn't being met. Looking closer, My'ala was also shocked to see the two guards had come equipped with bronze spears, which they levelled threateningly towards the source of Aurelius' sudden unease.

"Who're they talking to?" Su'la asked, tilting her head.

"I don't know… I can't *see*…"

Grumbling, My'ala took another step to the right, shifting out of her sister's shadow — and as she took in the full reality of the scene playing out before her, My'ala saw exactly who it was that the God-Elect was addressing.

Oh gods, no…

There were three figures, lingering in a huddle beneath one of the torch-poles, wearing nothing but their lower robes to hide what dignity they had left. Although they were stood completely still and were not being harried by gusts of wind, they seemed to sway and stumble about nonetheless, knocking each other's shoulders and holding each other aloft with the suspended light wedged between them.

Narrowing her eyes, My'ala made a closer inspection of their faces and saw an unusual aura resonating from them: a blind, careless bliss, shown through big, toothy smiles and twitching eyes that never lingered on any one thing for too long. When they spoke, the three individuals seemed to possess no control over how loud they were being, shouting raucously in one moment and whispering in near silence the next. They jeered at the crowds and stuck their tongues out, exhibiting senseless behaviour that seemed entirely without reason. To the common eye, one could say that they had become dispossessed of themselves, cavorting about like fiendish children as if they were completely—

Delirious…

My'ala tensed her toes, flexing her fingers at her sides.

Looking ahead again, she traced the contours of the figures' shadowy faces, and it was then that she saw something that she hadn't before: a thin trail of red juice clung around each of their mouths, spilling down their chins in strange channels.

At the sight of it, her heart caught in her chest, pushing up against her ribs like a caged animal.

These are the people who have been stealing from the bushes, she realised, taking a step forward. *These are the thieves… and they've lost control because of those berries.*

My'ala drew in a long breath; her skin went pale.

Because of their greed…

"Mi?" Su'la murmured, reaching out for her arm. "Mi, are you okay—"

"I have to get down there, *now*," My'ala replied forcefully, shrugging her sister off.

"It isn't our responsibility, Mi. They're handling it—"

"If we don't do something now, Su'la, then something *bad* is going to happen, and there's nothing we'll be able to do to stop—"

My'ala was drowned out suddenly by the sounds of shouting and the slurred ramblings of the three thieves, as one of them threw their hands up and blasphemed at the God-Elect, before turning in a half-circle and pacing off towards the greenery beyond—

Catching their foot on the torch-pole as they went, which

sent a shudder up into the flames above—

Causing the second figure to lurch to the side suddenly to keep their balance, the fire billowing and spitting above them as they leaned heavily on the pole—

Snap.

It happened in an instant.

A heartbeat.

A breath, so fragile.

The torch-pole broke in two, and the entire thing swung towards the ground in a single arc, hitting the dirt with a deafening thud—

As sparks were showered across the green foliage, scattering over the undergrowth beneath—

To catch alight and send it up in flames…

…as a fiery maw engulfed it all.

"*NO!*" My'ala screamed, shaking, lifting her hands to her mouth as her sister held her, her eyes awash with orange and yellow light as the vegetation crackled and burned, spreading rapidly out in all directions.

No…

There was screaming all around her, suddenly: people fleeing from the scene; those at their tents looking on in horror; children crying, clutching their hands over their eyes to make it all go away. Helpless and hapless and hopeless: the God-Elect stood with his guards pressed in against him, ushering him away from the inferno as he stared up in shock at the scene.

The fire raged, and burned on without any signs of stopping. The light was extraordinary, and harrowing. It ate at the night and submerged the stars.

Smoke swirled in the skies above. The scent of burning

clogged their nostrils, stinging their eyes as the wind swept through. At their feet, a number of tiny rodents scampered away from the scene, squeaking and chirping in fear as their home was ravaged by deadly flame.

Ravaged by greed, My'ala thought painfully, tears burning her eyes.

Ravaged by our greed, and our stupid ways...

She pushed away from Su'la's embrace and stood still for a moment, watching the fire. She could feel its heat on her face, and the light so bright that it hurt her mind. Regret flooded through her system: guilt and anger, too. There was nothing to do about it. Nothing she could do, nor control.

We've lost control...

With gritted teeth and tears in her eyes, she turned from the home they had ruined – *her* home; her hope – and faced the darkness of the desert beyond. Bitterness pulled up her neck; pain sunk its fangs into her gut.

It's lost... we've lost...

She started running.

XIV

OMENS

Dawn broke, and she was far away, in a place she would always remember.

Beneath a hibiscus bush, plying at the flowers with tiny hands. The soft thrum of hummingbird wings tapping in her ears. The glow of the sun in their walled garden, gleaming against the flower petals and the birds like shiny coins.

Her mother was there, and her sister too: their faces were young, and they smiled. She had never seen her ma so beautiful – it was as if she were gazing into the eyes of the gods themselves.

They pushed their faces between the branches of the hibiscus bush, peering at her like tiny mice emerging from their den. Then the bush rose on its trunk, stretching high above them like a canopy, until the sky was awash with leaves and petals and the hummingbirds darted around in their hundreds, every-thing aglow with the sun's yellow rays in dazzling, brilliant light.

Beneath the canopy, her sister and mother came to her, sitting by her side and huddling close, wrapping their arms around her. Their heads touched; their hair intertwined in tiny spirals. The moments stretched out like an eternity, as if never letting go.

And then she looked ahead, towards where their house would be, and saw a figure approach. He was young and spirited, in a workman's apron with dirt under his nails. Moving across the garden, he looked between the three of them, and produced an effortless smile that seemed to fill his whole face with awe and wonder.

Crouching down, he offered her his hand, lined with wrinkles like tiny streams racing out to sea.

Lifting a hand, she reached out towards him, wishing he was just that bit closer. His aura swelled in her mind and vibrated through her body; the memory was so strong that it filled her soul, seeping into her very bones. Looking up into his eyes; the tears forming in her own.

The open arms of an honest man.

Da, please don't go…

Dawn broke, and she was far away, in a place she would always remember. Now tainted with the pain of failure.

That she would find it very hard to forget.

My'ala opened her eyes a fraction like cracking a pair of stones, and saw the orange-red ripples of dawn ahead of her over the rising sands. A scratchy cloth lay beneath her head that she didn't remember putting there, tucking around her left ear and tickling against her lip. As she shifted her body slightly, she felt the blanket over her arms and legs, where it had kept her warm through the coldest part of night where even the hardiest souls could freeze. And yet, as with the cloth beneath her head protecting her skin from the sand, she couldn't remember putting it there.

Where even am I…

Peeling the blanket off of her robes – which she found were soaked with sweat, despite the cold winds – My'ala propped herself up on her elbow and craned her neck to look around. Her surroundings were indistinguishable, with the same rolling dunes and cloudless skies that she had become accustomed to over the previous weeks. The horizon was the colour of gemstones, with a number of different hues bleeding into each other as night was exchanged for the day. The stars were slowly banished, replaced with delicate blue tones like brushstrokes of thick paint. The wind lessened, and the warmth returned to the land, and nature pressed on like it always had regardless of the turmoil it faced. On reflection, My'ala could have mistaken the day for any other that had passed so far.

We're it not for the trail of grey smoke, that was, staining the skies to the north.

As she shifted her body more – her pulse rising suddenly – the smell of burning on her clothes caught in her nostrils and sent a shiver down her spine, conjuring a memory she wanted to wash from her skin and banish for as long as she could.

Her breath caught in her throat; she dragged the blanket off of her and pulled her knees up to her chin. Shivers jarred her body for several heartbeats as she adjusted to the change. As she steadied herself again — facing away from the trails of smoke — My'ala looked over to where she had been sleeping for a moment and——

"*Su'la?*" she mouthed, catching sight of her sister's figure beneath the rolls of the blanket, still completely lost to the world in a quiet and unruly slumber. The sight of her made My'ala shudder, her memory failing to piece things together.

What's she doing out here…

"She's been here all night, you know."

My'ala jumped, turning sharply to the right to find Othella stood next to them, looking north towards the trails of smoke. With her green hood down, her dark hair rippled in the wind, showcasing a dour expression.

"She followed you out here, trying to get you to turn around and go back to your tent… but you were almost in a trance, stumbling forwards with no knowledge of the world around you at all," the Muse explained, not turning her head. "Your sister followed you until you collapsed, so exhausted by your stress that you could do nothing but sleep. At first she was planning to use her own body warmth to keep you alive for the night, lying on top of you like a little cocoon…" She tilted her head down towards the blanket. "Luckily I arrived with a blanket to tuck you both in before you froze to death out here…"

My'ala looked between Othella and her sister, imagining Su'la cocooned around her, unmoving and——

No. She banished the thought. *She's alive, and so are you.*

Count your blessings.

"I… thank you for finding us out here," My'ala mumbled, hanging her head. "I feel so foolish."

"In times of great sorrow, we often let out emotions foul our better nature. Coming out here with nothing but the clothes on your back was foolish, yes… but the reasoning behind your disappearance was not."

"I couldn't bear to look at it any longer." The memory came, and the serpent in her stomach rattled its tail. "Everything we had worked so hard to create… gone, in a matter of *moments*."

Othella lowered her gaze. "One act of greed… and unthinkable consequences will follow."

"What's happened to the thieves who knocked the torch-pole over? The ones who ate the berries?"

"They've been detained for now… although no further action is expected. The God-Elect doesn't want to make an example of them – not when everyone's emotions are as frayed as they are."

My'ala nodded. "Good."

Othella raised an eyebrow in surprise. "Good?"

"They made a mistake… a *terrible* mistake, it's true, but a mistake nonetheless. Let them be reprimanded for their greed, but not for their actions under the influence of those berries… that's no precedent to set, if we wish to move forward."

By the slightest turn of the cheek, she saw the Muse smile. "How… *stoic* of you," Othella commented.

"It's how things should be done. I made my peace with vengeance long ago… the day my brother died." The words were sour on her tongue, but she swallowed them down and sighed. "When the news came, I could've quite easily demanded that we stand and fight those who had taken him from us. I could have let my reactions get the better of me, like a spark to a flame. But my family were hurting as much as I was, and people were afraid… and the consequences of someone's choice, whether right or wrong, should not mean the suffering of others in turn. We're better than that... and we need to be better than that now, moving forward."

Othella nodded towards the horizon. "You know... you're starting to sound like Artemis more and more every day."

At that – remembering his starry eyes and his mellow face – My'ala allowed herself a weak, fractious smile, a weight in her chest dislodging itself and sinking through her feet.

"I've always wanted to do people proud, especially where it matters most," she said, looking between her sister and Othella. "Whether that's you, my family, Artemis... or the people of Arbash as a whole. I want to honour those around me in everything I do, and give them answers when they're left with so many questions. I know anger won't solve what's happened, any more than vengeance will... and I know it won't benefit those around me if I give in to those feelings when they arise. So, where they need strength, *I* need to be stronger..." She rolled her fingers together, feeling her hands tingle. "That's the only way."

"You know that that's a lot of responsibility to place on one pair of shoulders, my dear. Especially one as young as yourself."

"But the burden is nothing, when the alternative is pain. These people that we travel with have looked to me for guidance ever since that day I spoke to them in Arbash... and I have no intention of letting them down now, especially when they need it the most."

Othella nodded, and didn't contest the point – she waved her hand out ahead of her, back towards their camp. "Well, speaking of that... you should know that the camp are planning to depart in the next turn or so, so it may be good to wake your sister and return to pack your things..."

My'ala heard the word *'depart'* and her heart cracked slightly, facing a reality she had been trying to avoid ever since the previous night. The smell of burning rekindled in her nostrils alongside it, burning over her mental wound. "So the oasis is ruined, then? It's really all gone?"

"They managed to get control of the blaze after a lot of hard work… but only once it had burned through nearly all of the green and polluted the waters with ash," the Muse replied solemnly. "When people awoke this morning, they found that what remained of the green had already started to wilt, and the waters were a murky grey for as far as the eye could see. It would probably take months for the oasis to return to how it was, and even that isn't a likely outcome. I'm sorry."

My'ala sucked her cheeks in and closed her eyes. "I see," she replied, lifting from her seat and brushing herself down, her mind now numb and disparaged. She regarded the Muse silently next to her, who only just decided to turn her head, revealing a starry eye that had been clouded with a milky grey.

For this is no time for the beauty of stars, My'ala considered in silence. *Only for the grey of storms, clouding everything in our path…*

"What are you thinking, my dear?" Othella inquired, looking down to her feet where Su'la continued to stir. "What will you do?"

Pulling her hair out of her face, My'ala looked from the smoke trails in the north to the shimmering horizon in the east, where the orange glow of dawn burned brightest and the dunes seemed to stretch on forever.

"Othella," My'ala said, watching the heat rise off of the sand.

"Yes, my dear?"

"Can you do me a favour, please?"

"Of course."

"Tell my sister when she wakes that I'm doing okay, and that she should return to our mother and help pack when she can. Tell her that I'll see them both soon… and will explain myself properly when the time is right."

"Okay… and what do you intend to do in the meantime?"

She paused. "I just need time to think… and some time away from everything. I'll follow alongside the camp once they all get moving, and I'll stay within sight of the main caravan, but… I just need to be alone now, please. It's best this way…"

Without waiting for an answer, My'ala turned to the east and started walking, placing one foot in front of the other.

She counted her steps to keep her mind busy, leaving Othella with her sister on the dune where she had collapsed, the blankets still warm from where she had slept.

Her body was tired, and her mind was exhausted, and there seemed to be no end in sight.

The sands stretched on ahead of her endlessly.

The only place left for her to go.

QUESTIONS

Sand and dust and stone. Rippling heat. Shifting earth. Soreness and aches and rashes. Fatigue, and exhaustion. Sweat leaking from every pore. The landscape stretching forever on, to a place she could not know. Hazy and unruly. Unforgiving and vast. Caring not for her plight, nor her wayward soul.

Questions, so many, lingering on the end of her tongue. Baying for blood; awaiting answers. Rising and falling like the sands of the Unknown.

Whistling out through parted lips:

What are we looking for in this place?

She crested one dune, and stumbled down the next, and released a dishevelled sigh. Her robes pulled tight around her head, holding her tight and still. Somewhere off to the left, the people of Arbash mirrored her steps, dragging their carts and belongings with them over the endless sea of sand. Just out of sight, but always there.

Watching.

Waiting.

So many people rely on us, now that we've nowhere to go. She dug her toes into the sand, flicking a cloud of dust skyward. *They expect answers from us… they expect us to know what to do, and where to go. They look to us with pleading eyes and open hands in prayer, hoping that we find a place out here somewhere.*

Anywhere we can.

Her jaw clenched and her teeth ground together; she balled her hands into fists and held them at her side.

But not really just 'anywhere', as we've found so far: we need somewhere with all the parts to make a whole, that can give us necessary shelter and a chance to begin again. A place where we can live at one with nature, and not be tempted by our bad intentions. Our greed, most of all.

Always our greed…

For a moment, she imagined the God-Elect at her side, donning his resplendent red-and-beige robes with their elegant gold trim, keeping pace with her with his piercing blue eyes fixed always on the horizon.

And what would you say to me, Aurelius, when I face these questions and long for their answers? What advice would you give to lead the way?

You'd tell me to find a place that provides for us, and allows us to prosper together. Somewhere that doesn't just give us what's necessary, but also provides opportunities to become something more. A place where we can become a 'society', as much as our individual selves.

She took a deep breath and shrugged at the thought, the sun

beating down against her cheeks.

And perhaps you're right, Aurelius: perhaps that is what we need the most. But where there is plenty, you will also find the covetous.

Those who are always wanting more…

Another dune rose and fell, and her mind shifted again. Descending a sandbank, she thought of her sister, her long hair blowing in the wind.

And you, Su'la: what would you say to me to comfort me when I need it most?

You'd tell me that a good foundation can build any great house, so long as you're willing to put the effort in to make it in the first place. Because nothing good is easy, and creating something takes time… and whether you have just enough to get by or plenty to spare, those first steps need to always be the strongest.

She smiled, imagining her sister's grin, and walked through a valley between two dunes.

But you cannot have stability in the long run, if the foundation cannot hold. We have seen a potential home that has offered us too little to begin with… and then one that was too fragile for us to ever touch.

And if that has taught us anything on this journey, it's that no matter where we go, our home must be strong enough to weather our mistakes, no matter how diligent we are. Because we are only mortal, after all.

And our flaws will always follow us…

Reaching the top of the next dune, she stopped and looked off to her left. There were people there – her people, she knew – charting their own course over the sands. There were hundreds of them, all desperate souls, swaying beneath the strength of the sun. Meandering on in a long line, towards a crest opposite her own.

Where a woman in green robes stood facing south, her single eye gleaming like a diamond.

She regarded the woman longingly, and the woman regarded her back. A vast understanding passed between them despite the distance, measured in a single glance. Sadness and mercy and guilt and pain; happiness and relief and love and bliss. Peering into each other's souls, to see what lay within.

Until the robed woman turned, bowing her head, and merged with the crowds just behind.

And what would you, Othella the Muse, tell me as I consider your question again? What wise words would you impart, if you were here at my side, with the wealth of the Known World at your fingertips?

You'd tell me that I must be cautious. You'd tell me to keep hope, and keep faith. You'd tell me that, no matter how many different places we encounter, and how many settlements we make, there will be one someday that is exactly what we need. A place that unites us, and sustains us; that reminds us of home but not as a replica; that allows us to innovate but not exploit; a place where we can be cautious of greed, and still live our lives to the full.

In an absent moment, she looked at her hands, tracing the lines across her palms.

But where is that, in such a vast and impossible place like this? And how are we supposed to find it, with how little we understand? We don't know the desert… we've not known the desert for generations at least. All we know is the safety of our walls, and the plots of our fields, and the springs that have brought us water since the dawn of time. We have routines and duties we've known our entire lives, that give us such purpose and momentum. And yet, out here, we're dislodged from all of that… stumbling about like children in a sandstorm, waiting for a perfect place to come.

She took a few steps, and several steps more, until she stood in a deep ridge with sand on all sides, completely isolated from the world. There was no wind nor sound around her; no voices or cries to be heard. There was just her singular presence, at the centre of it all.

When a thought came to her mind, eclipsing all other things.

Or maybe that's the point… maybe there isn't a perfect place out there. Maybe it was never there at all.

Because maybe the perfect place we've been longing for all this time… is the one we make for ourselves.

Her eyes bulged in their sockets, and a gasp escaped her lips, rippling over her skin and shaking the earth at her feet.

Tensing her chest, a knot began to unravel in the depths of her stomach, sliding out of place like a thick coil of rope that had refused to let go for so long——

As she peered down into the sand just ahead of her, heat flushing against her cheeks…

…and spied the piercing green eyes of a viper, with its tail twitching furiously at its back.

At first it was fear that came to her, alongside a desire to turn and run. Her legs became numb, and her knees locked, anticipating the serpent's strike. She flinched, almost looking away——

When the fear dissipated suddenly, dripping from her body like sweat, and in its place a fearlessness rose that defied every expectation she had.

She did not turn, nor look away. She didn't cower, nor whisper her prayers. Her eyes were locked with the viper's as its body coiled to strike, defiance burgeoning across her mind without a moment's doubt.

I've spent this entire journey with your burden, eating away at my fears and thoughts, she growled, clenching her fists. *I've let you control me, and unbalance me, and cloud my judgement at every turn. You've hurt me in ways I can hardly understand, hiding in my shadow for weeks.*

The viper bared its fangs.

But you won't haunt me any longer... I'm stronger than you are. My body and mind have no place for you. I must live my life with happiness and hope...

She snarled.

... and not with fear.

She opened her arms out wide, challenging the viper, making herself as large as possible as the tension thrummed in her head——

When the viper released a hiss suddenly and buried itself in the sand, disappearing beneath the surface.

Never to be seen again.

Watching the serpent's tail slip slowly out of sight, My'ala released a long breath and lowered her arms back to her sides. As she did so, a calmness swept through her body, banishing whatever stranglehold the serpent had had over her, letting an energy flow through her in waves like the pebbled cove back in Arbash.

A steadiness followed, relaxing the muscles around her heart – the muscles in her shoulders unravelled like balls of string.

The time for indecision is at an end, My'ala proclaimed, looking off to the north where her people continued their march across the sands, sheltering from the weight of the sun. *These people need us... they need our guidance and our will. Now is the time for strength, and direction.*

To find what we should look for, at last.

XV

BELIEF

When she returned to the people of Arbash, after several turns out on the dunes, she found them disconsolate and lost, dragging their feet and their belongings behind them with no perseverance left to spare. They glanced despondently at each other, with their hoods pulled tight over their heads. The elders shuffled along as if in mourning, while the children snuffled and wept with stray tears in their eyes. There was no solace for them anymore, it seemed: with the loss of two settlements in a matter of weeks — one of which had been destroyed completely by their own hands — they paced on over the dunes with little left to wish for, and little hope for whatever came next.

Sensing those feelings as she approached, My'ala stepped into the crowds with her hood cast down, letting her face shine and her hair flow freely at her back. She touched the arms and shoulders of those she passed, offering them sweet smiles and measured, kind words. At first they hardly acknowledged her, stuck in a sad trance of their own making, but after a while a few of them dared to look up and watched her drift elegantly past. Some of them simply looked on in wonder, while others mouthed a greeting in reply. Some even managed the faint remnants of smiles, standing slightly taller as it were.

My'ala wove her way between them like a threading needle, dipping in and out of crowds and opening them out in her wake. Suddenly people were looking up, and looking at each other with thoughtful eyes. People were mumbling, muttering words with mouths that had nearly lost the ability to speak. Here and there, the heartwarming sound of children laughing filled the air, drawing a few more smirks from the citizens as they trudged on into the Unknown.

Deep down, she knew it was not enough to repair the feelings of loss they had from leaving another oasis that could've been home. She knew it offered no insight as to what should come next, or where it was they should go. She knew she didn't have the words yet to answer the questions they were so desperate to ask. But even so, her presence amongst them still showed them one thing above it all: that they were still together as one, even after everything that had happened.

And it was their togetherness that would drive them forward, and ease their pain away.

Reminders of our unity, she thought with a swell of pride, trying to catch as many faces as she could as she manoeuvred towards the carts at the back. Glancing behind her for a moment, as the last few clusters of people passed her by, she saw with a great sense of relief that a number of people were now looking ahead rather than down at their feet, and the distinct background noise of conversation twittered away in her ears. It warmed her soul to hear it, like a burning hearth on a cold night: the people of Arbash had rekindled some of their old spirit, even if it only lasted a while.

It just shows how strong these people really are, when they overcome their own little fears, she thought with a broad, powerful smile. *They just need a reminder of who they are, and where they are.*

So we can deal with what comes next that much easier…

Looking ahead once more, with the stocky shapes of the canopied carts trundling over the sands towards her, My'ala picked one out in particular and acknowledged the gentle rise in her chest.

But before anything else, there's someone I need to see first. Someone I've been meaning to see all day…

She jogged over to the cart in question and skirted along its outer wall, dodging the rear wheels that cut deep grooves in the sand. Approaching the back gate, she hooked an arm around one of the canopy stirrups and swung herself up into the shade within——

Where she came face to face with her mother, who sat cross-legged at the other end of the cart.

My'ala gasped and nearly fell back out of the cart in shock. "Oh, ma, I'm… sorry, I didn't expect you to be here. Do you need me to go, or…?"

"No, no, Mi-Mi… please, stay," her mother replied, gesturing for her to take a seat. "We're family… we're all welcome here."

"Okay, if you're sure." My'ala placed herself down alongside her father's dormant figure, who was still nestled between the cloth sacks like a baby in its cot. She tried to avoid disturbing the surrounding area too much, for fear of jarring her father's body and causing any harm. As she looked over him, she saw his face had regained some more colour since she had last visited, and after a while she noticed a faint twitching in his fingers as he stirred in his long, distant sleep.

"How is he?" My'ala asked, reaching down to lift his hand and clasp it in her own. His fingers were warm and had the ripples of a pulse in them – faint, but distinctly there none-theless.

"He's doing better… the guards have said that he mumbles in his sleep now, which is nice, and there's movement behind his eyelids too… so that's good…" her mother replied, rolling her lips together to try and supress her emotions. With her heart aching, My'ala could hardly imagine the kind of thoughts going through her mother's mind, watching the man she loved try and wake up again. The constant waiting and checking in; the anxious nights without him by her side. There was no guarantee that he would return to them, or that he would be the same if he did. Thinking about it then, My'ala felt suddenly guilty that she hadn't acknowledged it sooner, and how she should've checked in on her ma more over the previous weeks.

Because I may be hurting, and struggling to handle everything that's going on… but she is too, even more so, and the person who usually cares for her is… well…

My'ala tightened her grip on her father's hand, and looked to her mother with a heartbroken smile.

"What is it, Mi?" she said softly, frailly.

"You're so strong, ma… I hope you know that," My'ala replied. "The support you've given us during this time is… it's phenomenal, and… I cannot thank you enough for it. And if you need anything at all, from Su'la or me, please just ask…

we're always here for you, ma. Always."

Despite her best efforts, her mother couldn't hold back the tears as they rippled down her cheeks in tiny rivers. She managed a smile – soft, delicate, like silk – and placed a hand over her chest. "Oh, Mi... it's nothing really... I just want to do what I can for you both... you and your sister..."

"But I know this affects you too, ma, and... we're here for you too, if you need it. We can't expect you to do this alone..."

"I appreciate it, Mi, I do... but you and your sister already give me everything I need, every day." She paused, her mouth curling at the edges. "Especially you, my beautiful girl... you give me so much courage."

My'ala frowned, puzzled. "What do you mean, ma? What do I do?"

"Oh Mi, I'm surprised you haven't seen it yourself: you're usually so insightful!"

"Seen *what*? What are you talking about?"

"Why you come here, nearly every day no matter how busy you are... and sit with him as you do now, holding his hand," she explained, looking down at their father's still, resting face. "It's something you don't realise, I think, because of how occupied you are with trying to answer all of these big quest-ions you have about the world and our place in it. You're out there on the sands, looking everywhere and asking everyone for what you should be looking for in life to find our next home... when really, it's been in front of you all along." She reached down, and brushed a hand against their father's cheek. "It's the one thing you've always held closest to you, and the one thing that never gives up hope..."

Her mother looked deep into her eyes – her gaze spoke a thousand words.

"…*family*."

My'ala blinked, looking between her mother and the dormant shape of her father. Her breath caught in her throat; her heart was suddenly racing.

A caravan of thoughts rolled through her mind, replaying her mother's words.

My family were the ones that guided me through the turmoil of leaving Arbash…

When I thought of what made my house a home with Othella, it wasn't the memory of a specific event: it was because my family were there with me too…

When I had that vision this morning, it was of my family in my favourite place, with all of us together…

And when I ever need help or need to talk alone, I always come back here to see da, because whenever the day is up or the storm closes in, you go to the place you feel safest…

Home.

Her heartbeat resounded in her chest, echoing through her body. The air around her head seemed to lose pressure, prickling in her ears. Her father's hand twitched in her grasp, as if registering her thoughts through her touch.

Outside of the canopy – in the real and tangible world beyond – a number of shouts rang out all of a sudden from somewhere far ahead of them, followed by several horn blasts from the God-Elect's roving scouts. In response, the cart they were in jolted forward abruptly, driven by the thought of something new in the sandy oblivion ahead.

"Oo, it seems they've found something… how about that," her mother said innocently, turning her ear to the fore. "And, by the sound of the commotion, it must be another oasis or something…"

Found something… an oasis…

My'ala lifted a hand and slapped herself across the cheek, forcing a breath from her mouth as she returned to the real world once again. Her breath hitched in her chest for a moment, as she looked across the cart at her mother and lifted from her seat.

"Ma, come with me now… we haven't got much time," she said frantically, offering out a hand and turning towards the back of the cart.

Her mother's eyes opened wider, an uneasy confusion on her face. "Wha… Mi, what are you——?"

"Just trust me… please."

Staring at her, completely dumbfounded but with no other choice, My'ala's mother clasped her hand and lifted to a stoop, stepping carefully over her father's body.

"What are you planning on doing, Mi? Where are we going?"

My'ala didn't respond at first – instead, she looked behind her and gave a wry smile.

"We're gonna show them what home is, of course," she exclaimed, tugging at her arm. "Now come on, let's go!"

XVII

FAMILY

In the glory of the midday sun, with their cowls hiding their faces from the worst of the heat, the people of Arbash gathered together like a flock of birds with bright, expect-ant eyes. Flanked by the baggage carts, they spread out in a semi-circle on a flat ridge of the dune, overlooking whatever the scouts had discovered beyond. At their head — stood atop one of the carts with his arms opened wide — Aurelius and his personal guards stood preparing a first address, assessing the mistakes of the past and declaring the return of a brighter future.

It was a prophetic scene, with the needy hands of the many taking refuge in the words of the few. Sobering, considering the desperation involved, with rapidly-dwindling rations and a severe lack of water. For many of those gathered on the dune's plateau beneath the sun, the occasion marked a turning point that had crept up on them so subtly: a steadily rising tide, pulling up the beach in tiny increments. The slow realisation that, in the grand scheme of things, whatever lay before them over the lip of the dune would be one of the last chances they had of salvation. A final opportunity to find a place called home.

A final opportunity to survive.

So the people of Arbash stood with bated breath, awaiting their leader's words. They stood with hands closed in prayer, muttering words through cracked lips like statues possessed. They had one chance to make things right; one chance to put the failures of the past behind them.

And along one edge, skirting the crowds with her mother latched onto her hand, My'ala approached the front of the crowds with a determined look in her eye.

Knowing what she had to do.

"Come on, ma: we're nearly there!" she cried, looking back to see her bedraggled mother struggling to keep up, a redness in her cheeks betraying whatever strength remained in her smile. "Not far now, just keep moving!"

Looking to her left, My'ala watched her fellow citizens as she frantically passed them by, their heads turning and their pupils igniting as they wondered what she planned to do. They were curious and wistful as they watched her go, remembering how her presence had uplifted them earlier that day, with the simplest act of meeting their eye. Their backs straightened at the memory; their shoulders opened wide. My'ala managed to smile at a few of them where she could, and heard her mother mumble a few greetings at her back, but her focus remained on the path ahead, the words she wanted to say palpable on her lips and refusing to let her go.

Only a short distance now, she thought, banking left suddenly as she reached the corner of the crowds, the imposing wooden baggage carts penning them in like goats. Along the ridge of the plateau ahead of her, she spied the God-Elect and his guards atop their makeshift platform, discussing something in hushed voices with nervous looks in their eyes. As she rounded the edge of the crowd and began her swift approach, one of the guards poked his head up like a sand-fox and frowned in her direction, gaining the attention of Aurelius who looked towards her too.

My'ala managed a tired smile.

We're almost there—

"Mi, *look!*"

It was her mother's voice, calling out from just behind her: an exclamation of surprise, with a hint of joy in the mix.

Despite her dogged focus on the platform ahead, and the words that seem to tingle on her tongue like worms, she was dragged backwards suddenly by her mother's clasping hand, and turned towards the ridge on her right-hand side—

Where she was beholden to a sight that made her heart catch in her chest, fizzing out to her fingertips in tiny ripples.

There was a watering hole down there of beautiful blue, with reed beds and grasses clinging to its edges. There were trees, spindly and thin on the far bank, with tiny green buds and small hanging fruits. There were bushels and thick-stemmed plants, with jets of green leaves at their pinnacles. There were broken stone blocks and cracked wooden struts, forming the remains of ancient buildings at its edges.

There was nothing unique about it at first glance: nothing to suggest it was any different than any other place they had found. It was a water-source, out on the sands, raising life from its muddied banks. Creatures lived there, and perhaps people had once too. It was, My'ala imagined, just like every other oasis there was to find, out in the vastness of the Unknown.

But something about it embedded in her soul, and nestled there a hatchling beneath their mother's wing. Something that transcended all other thoughts she possessed, in ways that she hadn't felt before. It wasn't something that reminded her of the first watering hole, or the luscious green they experienced at the second. It possessed traits from both of those places, but never in the same ways. And, as she thought on it further, My'ala soon realised that the memories it conjured were different altogether.

It reminds me of the fields... outside Arbash, she gasped, approaching the platform cart. *A place that I never thought could be replicated out here...*

She looked back to her mother with wonder in her eyes.

A place that lives long in my memories...

Something opened in her soul.

A place that reminds me of home.

Turning ahead again, My'ala hoisted herself up onto the rear gate of the cart and clambered onto the wooden platform beyond, struggling to peel her eyes away from the oasis on her right. As she lifted to a stand, she came face to face with the dour expressions of the guards, and the utterly perplexed look of Aurelius huddled in between them.

"My'ala, are... is everything okay?" he asked, stepping in closer to keep his voice low. "I thought you were with your parents...?"

"I am... sort of," My'ala replied, stepping aside and gesturing down to her mother, who gave an awkward wave. "One of them, at least."

"I see, yes, but... how come you're here? I'm about to give an address to everyone... has something happened?"

"No, no, nothing has happened, I just..." Drawing in a long breath, she met Aurelius' eyes and placed a hand to her chest. "I need to say something to them... to all these people, before we all descend upon this new haven and try to make it our own. Because... I've done a lot of thinking and... there's just something I need to say..."

Aurelius nodded his head, considering. "This is highly unorthodox, you know..."

"I know it is, I know, just... *please*, Aurelius," My'ala begged, trying to keep the worry from her voice. "I wouldn't be asking to do this if it wasn't important, I promise you."

Without voicing his reply, the God-Elect glanced from the people on his right to the oasis over the ridge on his left, the cogs visibly turning in his mind as he weighed up his options. Left waiting, My'ala clenched and unclenched her hands opposite him, feeling her pulse rise steadily in her chest.

Time was of the essence; time seemed to stretch on for an eternity. The people below them shuffled on the spot and looked up to the platform where they stood, wondering what was going on and waiting for what they had to say—

"Okay," Aurelius said abruptly, placing a hand on My'ala's shoulder. "Okay, I... I'm trusting you with this. You have the floor..." He squared his jaw, bowing his head. "Now make it *count*."

He stepped back suddenly – waving away the consternations of his two personal guards – and left My'ala stood alone before the amassed people of Arbash, the sun beating down powerfully overhead as the heat rose in her neck.

You have the floor, she breathed.

Now make it count…

Turning to them – a dizziness swimming in her head – she looked between their faces for a moment, her gaze dancing across the crowds, picking out people she knew and those she recognised and even those she had never seen before. Their quizzical expressions beneath heavy cowls; children on their parents' shoulders, and elders hanging on to wobbly canes. All of them expectant, and desperate, and exhausted. From the vantage point, she could see across their entire span, gathered along the plateau of the dune.

These stoic people, who have endured so much and lost so much and yet still hold their heads high, she acknowledged, the corners of her mouth slowly curling into a smile. *These people who have traversed vast deserts, just like their ancestors generations before, in search of a new place to make their own. People who have faced great challenges, and have overcome great adversity. The survivors, in all this.*

The heroes, too.

She continued looking across their faces, acknowledging the tiny flickers of hope rekindling in their eyes, when My'ala finally drew her attention to the rear of the crowds—

To find Othella and her sister there, stood side by side, watching her with big smiles and the warm glow of pride. Su'la waved to her and put her thumbs up; the Muse bowed her head slowly, and gestured for her to begin.

They're here for me, as they have been all along, My'ala thought, a mellowness resonating from her heart. She let out a long breath and opened her hands out at her sides. *They've never stopped believing in me.*

So I guess it's time to do them proud.

"Citizens of Arbash! Nomads of the Unknown!" she cried, lifting her hands above her head. "Lend me your ears!"

From the forefront of the crowds to the sparse congregations at the rear, all eyes turned to her, shielding their eyes from the sun.

"We are survivors, all of us here, and we have endured so much on our journey from the walls of our homeland! We have rejoiced, and we have suffered, and we have prevailed! We have shown kindness, and tolerance, and love! We have grown angry, and shown our mercy… and have been proven better for it!"

At her words, a few idle faces turned to one side, where the thieves who had stolen the berries were still chained to the carts, listening on with their heads hung low.

"And now… here, in this beautiful place we have found… we must face a new choice, even greater than any we've faced so far!" she bellowed, one of her hands sweeping back towards the haven behind her. "Because we have encountered many things on our journey so far… and all of them have failed us in some way, leading us to this desperate point. We found a watering hole that could not sustain our thirst; that gave up on us, and forced us to flee. We found a beautiful green paradise, with an abundance beyond our wildest dreams… but its wealth proved far too fragile – and its life-force, far too sensitive – for the very real, natural errors we carry with us as people every day. And, standing before you as I do now, I want to say that I do not believe it was the actions of the few that caused that downfall to occur… but instead, it was caused by all of us, the moment we set foot on its sands…"

A number of disapproving grumbles and nods of agreement rippled through the crowd in equal measure – nervously,

My'ala drew their attention back, and placed a hand on her chest.

"Now, it took me some time to realise that, and to allow that into my heart, as I imagine it will for you too… but if we're honest with ourselves, we could have never lived freely in a place so delicate, when our hands are often too firm to care," she admitted, nodding her head. "Because we are imperfect, as people, and we all have a part to play. We often realise our mistakes only after we've made them, when the good we have sought has gone. We are often misguided by our emotions, or the less pleasant parts of our nature – but that, too, is an element of who we are, as much as breathing and sleeping are. We are complex, and we are flawed… and things will go wrong, sometimes, no matter how ideal life seems to be." She stood to one side, opening up a space between the people and the new oasis. "We have spent so much of our journey into the Unknown so far looking for somewhere that has everything we need. Looking for something perfect, to hold us in place forever. But now, after some time thinking… I don't believe a place like that exists for us at all… and I don't think it ever did, either."

She took a deep breath, watching a wash of concern cross the faces of those beneath her.

"But I also think it's better that way, for all of us… *together*," she continued. "Because what we have sought so far, in this wild and volatile land, is a perfect place that just falls into our laps: a pair of boots that fit just right, by luck more than judgement." She raised a finger like an orator. "But that isn't how the world works! That isn't what this life is meant to be! And we shouldn't expect it to be, either!" She pointed off behind them, out west across the Unknown. "Our home – our city –

was built for us, it's true… but we *made* Arbash what it was, with our own hands and our own words. Arbash was so much more than its physical parts: it was all of our separate lives and interactions, flowing freely day-by-day, that made it into the home we now remember so fondly. *Connection*, and our flaws and triumphs, are what made Arbash *home*." She paused. "And in time – slowly, but surely – I believe that an oasis like the one behind me can become our home too, just like Arbash was before it… but only if we truly *work* for it, and remember who we are at our *core*."

Opening a hand out next to her, My'ala leaned back and grasped the God-Elect's hand, pulling him in next to her and looking across with a smile.

"We are friends, and colleagues, and we care for each other with all our hearts…"

Tilting her head, she gestured to her mother stood timidly to the side of the cart, and gave her a wink.

"We are mothers, and daughters, and we love each other more than words can do justice for…"

Lifting her arms, she cradled the entire crowd before her.

"We are workers, and farmers, and elders. We are siblings, and teachers, and carers. We are guardians, and providers; we bring peace and order, and stability. We do what is necessary for those we care about, and do whatever we can for everyone else. Because we are all bonded together at heart, whether by blood or by spirit. We are part of a unified whole, that has worked so hard together to become something new. It is the reason we have made it this far, and overcome so much, and traversed this impossible place with smiles still on our faces…"

She let a single tear roll down her cheek.

"Because what we need most in life, no matter where we are

or what we do… is *family,* above all else," she said softly, letting her voice carry on the wind. "And it is in our family, together as one, that we shall prevail against all odds, and keep the hope alive in our hearts… and turn this new haven into something magical."

She took a deep, soulful breath.

"Something… that looks like *home.*"

From atop the platform of the cart, with fresh air in her lungs and tiny teardrops in her eyes, My'ala looked across the crowds of the people of Arbash and saw a change come over them.

People looked to each other, and smiled, and embraced with tender hands. The young put their arms around the elderly, who laughed and rattled their canes. Children reached down from their parents' shoulders and hugged their heads, their tiny infant hands holding on gently. Workers and farmers locked arms, as their sons and daughters huddled together and giggled with glee.

A togetherness seeped out amongst them: a unity formed in bright eyes and kind gestures and words of thanks and grace. From every corner of the crowd, right to the very back, people hugged and laughed and recalled fond memories with a happiness they'd thought they'd lost long ago. Hope shone brightly between them, beneath their cowls and over their shoulders, beating like an aura from their souls.

A family, one and all, reminded of their humanity again.

Together, always, for better or for worse, My'ala thought.

This is all we need.

And as she looked across the crowds, and a lovingness swept through her like sea waves, she caught sight of something out of the corner of her eye, approaching the cart slowly on her left.

And when she looked there to see who it was, everything else seemed to stop, and the world had never seemed so beautiful.

Their movements were stiff and slow, balancing against a walking stick as they trudged their way over the sand. Their breathing was thin, but holding steady, and their face was lined with wrinkles.

They reached the rear gate of the cart and embraced My'ala's mother, who stood there shaking with tears in her eyes, muttering breathless prayers. With some help from the God-Elect's guards, and a boost from My'ala's mother, the figure clambered up onto the wooden platform and stood next to her with shiny brown eyes.

The most beautiful sight she had ever seen.

"Hey, Mi," her father said.

Her breath hitched in her throat; tears streamed from her eyes. "Hey, da," she mumbled, her hands shivering.

He reached over and brushed her cheek, stroking her face with wrinkled hands. His eyes looked across the crowds ahead of them, and then back to her. "You did all of this?"

"Yea... yea I did."

He offered a rich, wonderful smile. "I knew you could do it, Mi." He took her hand in his own, clasping it like a baby's. "I'm so *proud* of you."

My'ala felt the warmth in his hands – the pulse beating happily in his fingers – and clenched her hand around his as if she would never let go again.

"I love you, da..."

"I love you too, Mi... and no matter what happens, I always will."

At that, he turned from her to the crowds, and lifted their

hands together.

"For family," he whispered, like stardust.

On her opposite side, Aurelius hefted their hands skywards and gave her a joyful grin.

"For *family*!" he cried with an almighty cheer.

And ahead of them, across the entire plateau, the citizens of Arbash raised their hands in unison, clasped together, blood and spirit, and bellowed loud at the top of their voices for the entire Unknown to hear…

"*For family!*"

XVIII

HOME

The day passed, and evening followed, and the people of Arbash went to work building their settlement once again. Tents were erected, and canopies were propped in place, and fireplaces were set in neat little pits. Water was passed out, and flat stones were drawn up as seats, and torches were lit on tall poles as the light began to fail.

But this time, things were different – *they*, as a people, were different. The mistakes of the past were ever-present in their minds, and the hopes for the future burned bright in their souls. Everything was done based on the needs of the many, and every decision was made with unanimous approval. Land was allocated fairly. Water was distributed evenly. Food supplies were passed around willingly, so everyone ate their fill. None were left behind, and none were left longing.

Because they were a family, after all, and that's what families did for each other.

It would be a long process, they knew, and new challenges would arise at every turn. There would be mishaps, to begin with, and there would be pain. People would give in to their less-amenable natures, and be tempted to do wrong in times of need. But, with a unity that they had not possessed before, the people of Arbash knew that, and embraced it all the way.

Because their world was an imperfect one, and as its mirror image, so were they. Like the dunes they had crossed – unchanging, yet always shifting – the path ahead was impossible to know, but was always in sight. And whatever they faced on that path, and whatever dangers lurked over the next ridge, they knew that they would prevail nonetheless.

Because when they did, they did so together.

Family, one and all.

Walking through the camp at dusk, with the orange-red glow of the setting sun ahead of her in the west, My'ala looked around her at her fellow citizens, and saw the winds of change begin to blow through.

Passing one tent with a family sat around a campfire, she saw a group of young men drift by and offer handfuls of dry fruits with a smile, which two rosy-cheeked children took graciously from them, remembering their thank-you's as they waved them goodbye.

On her other side, she spied an elderly couple struggling to get their fire lit, their hands shaking dramatically with the cold – when a young lady carrying a basket stepped under their canopy and huddled down next to them, offering to help and giving them instructions with gently, shiny eyes.

Further ahead, she saw another fire had been constructed out in the open with the stars. Around it, a dozen or so children sat with their legs crossed, peering up into the vast night sky as an older man explained the constellations. They asked their questions, and the man gave his replies, taking them on a magnificent journey across the vast and impossible Beyond.

Passing them by – hearing the man's extravagant tales – My'ala couldn't help but smile, and as she stepped into the light of the campfire the old man looked across and waved, drawing smiles and looks of wonder from the children all around him.

Our connections are built on the stories we hear as children, she considered, waving back and continuing on through the camp towards the sunset. *Whether that's from our parents as we settle into bed... or our teachers in the learning halls of school... it's those stories that remind us of who we are, and where we belong in this life.*

Because those children may not remember much of our journey across the sands when they grow older. They may not remember much of the turmoil we've been through, getting here.

But what they will remember, hopefully, is that once everything had settled, and we made camp one last time... one man sat with them, all together, and talked to them about the stars.

She took a final glance back, hearing the children burst out with laughter.

And that, right there... makes this all worth it.

Approaching the outer reaches of their camp – where the dunes rose steeply onto the plateau they had gathered on earlier that day – My'ala peered up into the hazy orange light and spied several figures at its highest point, gathered close together. Even from the bottom of the sandbank, with their bodies as little more than shadows, My'ala knew immediately who they were, and found a warmth in her heart at their presence.

She ascended the dune-side slowly, letting her feet submerge into the sand and run like water between her toes. Behind her, their new settlement sprawled out around the bowl of the oasis, quiet and content with the musings of conversation twinkling like wind-chimes. There was a peace to it that she hadn't seen before; a contentment that hadn't been truly present in their previous attempts to create a home.

Because they understand what it all means now, and what's important for it to survive, My'ala considered. *Togetherness, and unity…*

Reaching the plateau, she stepped forward and joined the others, looking out on the beautiful sunset burning bright on the horizon beyond.

And family, one and all.

"We wondered when you'd get here, my sweet," her mother said, her long, flowing dress dancing in the wind like a delicate ceremonial veil.

"You took your time!" Su'la added, offering a mischievous smirk. "I was getting rather bored."

"Now Su'la, come along," her father said with a knowing smile, stood between them with his cane propped under his right shoulder. "I think what your sister is *trying* to say… is that it's nice to have you here with us, Mi, now that you've finished to tending to your things."

"It's nice to be here with you guys too… it's really nice," My'ala replied, placing a hand on her father's back, watching the fiery glow of the sinking sun ahead. "It's beautiful here."

"It is," Othella replied on her opposite side, her green hood drawn down and her hair fluttering angelically in the breeze. "I've lived out on these sands for many, many years… and I can safely say that sights like these *never* get old."

"And this is our home now," her father exclaimed. "A place like this… blessed with sunsets like these."

"A truly wonderful thing indeed."

They stood in silence for a while, shoulder to shoulder, as the sun passed beyond the horizon inch-by-inch. Over their heads, the orange and red of fading dusk gave way to the blue and purple of twilight.

"I've… been wanting to apologise to you, Othella, for how I treated you before, and for everything that has happened between us so far," her father spoke up suddenly, lowering his gaze in shame. "I should have never spoken to you like I did in the God-Elect's tent that night, or raised my voice at you in the way that I did. And as much as I could give any number of excuses as to why I behaved in the way that I did… in the end, that doesn't really matter. My behaviour was poor, and my reaction was wrong… and I am truly sorry for the whole affair."

"Well… consider your apology accepted, Mr Busskar, and also consider yourself entirely forgiven for what happened at the feast that night," Othella replied, pursing her lips. "And, as we're in this position and we're all here together… I also want to apologise for the part I played in the whole mess, and for not being open with you all about my time in conversation with My'ala here. I know it contributed to a lot of the ill-feeling experienced on that night, and I assure you that I *never* intended for that to happen—"

"But I think, if we're honest with ourselves… we've *all* made mistakes and done things we didn't mean to on this journey, wouldn't you say?" Su'la interrupted. "We all have things we feel guilty about, or feel we should apologise for —

some of us perhaps more so than others. But, it's as My'ala said earlier: we have all made mistakes, and will continue to make mistakes in the future… because that's how we are as *people*. We are flawed by our very nature, and we do things wrong without meaning to… but it's our mercy and forgiveness in the face of that, that really showcases our strength as individuals."

"Life's too short to hold on to animosity," her father added, nodding his head slowly. "And if you ask me, Othella… even though there were some mistakes in the beginning, and we most *certainly* got off on the wrong foot at the start… you did an excellent job of helping us find this place, and looking after My'ala in my absence. So… thank you for that, and everything you've done for us." Stepping past My'ala, he offered a hand out to the Muse. "You're the hero in all of our stories, I'd say."

Studying her father's hand, and the honest expression of the man himself, My'ala watched Othella pull her sleeve up and clasp his outstretched hand, shaking it firmly with a delicate bow and an all-encompassing smile.

"And you have all made this experience truly special for me, on this strange little adventure we've been on," the Muse replied, passing her smile down the row to her mother and sister. "So, you have my thanks too… I shall remember this time fondly, and wish you all the best in your new home."

My'ala bristled then, and felt her heart sink in her chest. A realisation came to her so suddenly that her legs almost gave out beneath her.

"So… this is it, then?" she mouthed, peering up at the starlit eye. "This is… the end?"

Stood next to her, like a statue of the gods above, Othella rolled her lips together and looked to My'ala's father. With a nod, she placed a hand on My'ala's shoulder and guided her several steps forward, so they were stood alone on the plateau with the red sun coating their robes.

There, the Muse turned to her, clasping her hands in front of her. "Hello, My'ala," she said softly.

"Hi Othella," she replied, rolling her tongue across the roof of her mouth. "So... this is it?"

Othella nodded. "This is it for us, yes."

My'ala looked down at the palms of her hands, and sighed. "I knew this day would come eventually... but I guess that doesn't make it any easier when it finally arrives."

"That's true, yes... but the sadness you feel at the journey's end, only shows how much joy the journey brought." Stretching an arm out, she opened her hand out towards the sun — to the west, and the vast expanse they had travelled across. "We've been through a lot over these past few weeks, out on the sands together. We've learned a lot, and laughed a lot... and cried a lot, too. We've conquered things that would've buried you once before, and experienced things that will live with you for a lifetime. And I think those are things that we'll cherish, in what comes next... I know I will."

"But, if you go, then... what if I need you, or need advice? What if I don't know the way anymore?"

Othella smiled, and gestured behind her — back towards My'ala's family, stood watching the sunset together. "Like you said to your people, earlier today: you have everything you need right here, in the people who make life worth living," she said softly. "They need you, as much as you need them... never forget that."

My'ala nodded, uncertain on her own feet. "How will I know if we're going in the right direction, though? How will I know if this is the right place for us?"

"Oh, my dear… you already *know* this is the right place for you. I can see it in your eyes…" – she reached over and tapped My'ala's chest, right over her heart – "…all you have to do now, is *prove it.*"

My'ala stepped forward and wrapped her arms around Othella, her hands braced against the soft cloth robes. The Muse did likewise, as My'ala smelt spices and flowers and wistful smells on the wanderer's long, shimmering hair. Reminding her of life before and the joys of life to come. A memory that she would hold forever.

To nurture, and to love.

"Thank you for everything, Othella," My'ala said as they parted again, wiping a stray tear from her eye. "It's been a true pleasure to have met you, and to have had you join us on our journey."

"The pleasure's all mine, My'ala," the Muse replied with a glint in her eye. "You're a remarkable woman, and a born leader, and you have such strength and courage in you. It's been my honour to follow you to this beautiful place… and I wish you many long and prosperous years ahead." She held My'ala's shoulders, and smiled.

"Artemis would be *proud*, to see who you've become… and even though him and I will both become a memory, we'll still be with you, always… up, in the *stars.*"

Turning from her with a flush of her green robes – offering a final wave to her family stood at the edge of the plateau beyond – Othella walked off towards the setting sun, basking in glorious light.

My'ala watched her go, a smile plastered to her face with tears threatening in her eyes. The woman she had found at an ancient well, in a tent beneath a gnarled old bush. The woman who had joined them, and helped them, and became one of them as if she had been there all along. The woman who had guided them, and helped them overcome. The woman with the starlit eye.

Who had found them a place to call home.

And as the sun slipped below the western horizon, and her figure became little more than a shadow, a flash of shimmering green light scattered across the night sky.

And Othella the Muse, was gone.

So, another chapter ends, My'ala thought, watching the stars above. Looking behind her, she saw her family on the ridge, with their new home illuminated just beyond.

And now, together as one...

A new chapter begins.

Epilogue

THE JADE SUN

Three Days Later...

At the edge of the camp, with the afternoon sun setting at their backs, the two builders looked down on the broken blocks of stone and frowned, their hands firmly planted on their hips. They had been busy over the previous few days, helping to lay the foundations for various small dwellings around the edge of the watering hole. It had been back-breaking work, trying to heft the stones around to make neat pontoons, but the majority of the work had been done in good time.

And now, all they had to do was work out what to do with the rest.

"What does the God-Elect want done with it again?" one of

them asked, scratching at a knot of hair sprouting from his chin.

"As far as I'm aware, he just wants us to move it," the other replied, adjusting his work apron pre-emptively. "His Highness was rather light on details, as far as I recall."

"Where do you reckon we should move it to? Out of the way of the main camp, I suppose."

"I reckon we stick it with the other supplies out along the western sandbank. That way it can keep out of people's way and not be an eyesore anymore."

"Sounds good to me." He clapped his hands together. "Right, best get to it, then!"

Hunkering down on either side of the first block – which was as large as a cart wheel, and perhaps four times as heavy – the two men grasped the eroded edges and sucked deep breaths through their teeth. Counting down from three, they strained the muscles in their legs and hoisted the stone away, dragging it to one side before setting it down a short distance away.

"This is gonna be hard work," the one with the small beard grumbled.

"You don't say?" the other replied.

Stretching out their backs, they returned to the broken stone pile and assessed their next move. The builder with the apron took a step forward and knelt on one of the blocks, brushing away some of the sand that had sat beneath the stone they moved—

"Whoa!" he exclaimed, stumbling back in shock.

"What? What is it?" His colleague stumbled forward and elbowed his way in next him, peering over the lip of the stone to see what the fuss was about. "What is—"

His face paled suddenly; a gulp forced its way down his throat.

"Oh…"

The builder with the apron lifted to a stand, brushing his hands off. He tapped his colleague on the shoulder. "Hey, lad?"

The other builder shuddered and looked up at him, his eyes big and white like an owl's. "Y-yes?"

"Go fetch the God-Elect, will you? Get some air while you're at it." Adjusting his apron again, he looked down at the pit of sand. "And tell him to bring that lady with her too… the one with all the answers."

A shudder passed through him.

Because we might be needing some…

My'ala and the God-Elect had listened to the builders' story half-heartedly at first, wondering why they had been summoned away from their duties to listen to two men talk about stones. Admittedly, the men had taken an indirect approach with their recount, and had explained a number of extra details that could have been left unsaid — but once they mentioned what they had found beneath the first huge slab, My'ala and Aurelius had exchanged questioning looks and demanded to see it at once.

"We don't know who's it is, or how long it's been there," the builder with the apron explained, pacing over to the pile of stones where they had made their discovery. "All we do know is that it's been trapped under there for a *very* long time…"

Taking the lead, My'ala stepped in close and squat down over the blocks, wiping some of the sand away that had already started to build up. As she removed more of the substrate, and uncovered what it was that had caused the builders such surprise, she locked her hand around it without any fuss and wrenched it free from its resting place.

Well, how about that...

It was a bone of some sort, was all that My'ala could ascertain: a single, thin piece with a joint on one end, and a jagged edge on the inner side that may have once been connected to something else.

"Well, it's definitely what you two said it was..." My'ala said, turning back to Aurelius and the builders. "Any idea what part of the body it's from?"

The builders looked to each other and shrugged awkwardly, unsure of what to say — the God-Elect, meanwhile, inspected it closer and began to nod his head.

"It looks like a forearm bone," he deduced, pointing at his elbow and his wrist, "connecting these two parts. Which, theoretically, means there's a hand somewhere in there too."

Curious about the God-Elect's assumption, My'ala turned back to the gap in the stones and reached down into the sand, her fingers tracing over shrapnel and debris before finding another long, thin object.

Testing its leverage, she lifted her hand and plucked it out from its resting place, holding it up to the dusky light for all of those present to see.

As she studied it, however, her face furrowed with a frown. "Is it just me," she exclaimed, "or is this the *exact* same bone?"

The God-Elect took another step forward, swapping his gaze between the two bones. "It is, yes," he confirmed, his head tilting. "Although the one you've just found is significantly smaller and more dense than the first, by the look of it."

"What does that mean?"

"It means that we're not actually looking at one body, but

rather *two* – and by my estimation, one of them belongs to a child, and the other is a woman." He paused. "Maybe it's the bodies of a mother and son, or an older sister and brother perhaps?"

My'ala considered the options – as Aurelius reeled off a number of facts, including the unverifiable nature of old bones – when something flickered to life in the deepest reaches of her memory, catching light and setting a blaze that reached the very forefront of her mind.

A mother and child, out in the desert... a storm, swallowing an oasis...

A house collapsing, two people trapped inside—

My'ala gasped and dropped the bones; the builder with the beard leapt backwards in shock.

"What is it?" Aurelius asked, suddenly alert. "What happened?"

"I... I know who these people *are*..." she replied, studying her hands. She turned to the God-Elect and the builders, her eyes alive with activity.

"Gather as many able-bodied people as you can, *now!*"

Several turns came and went; dusk began to fall.

And beneath a stack of stones on the outskirts of an oasis, the remains of a woman and child were found.

Holding them in her hands as she had wrapped them in pieces of cloth, My'ala had hardly believed an entire person could be made up of such a small amount of bones. With the intricacies of every person, and the inexplicable cycle of life they endured year on year, she had thought that they would be made of something more beneath the skin.

But in the end, we are all nothing more than bones, she had thought as she folded the last wrap of cloth.

And even bones deserve the honour of being buried.

With the help of a few of the builders who had stayed behind with her, My'ala and the God-Elect had carried the piles of bones up the steep sandbank to the west, up onto the plateau above where the desert could be seen for miles around. The sun had been sinking rapidly by then, bathing the world in orange and red hues, and she knew that time would be of the essence if she was to get things done in time.

So, with their bare hands, they had clawed at the sand and dirt to build tiny graves for the bodies, lowering the remains down into the earth where they could finally be at peace. Small rocks and pebbles from the shore of the watering hole were brought up as well, carried in baskets by strong individuals doing their best for their fellow man. My'ala ordered for them to be laid out over the surface of the graves until they covered every inch of the mound – and, after much toil battling against the chill winds, the final stone was laid down at last.

And so their journey is complete.

Sitting on the cool sand with the graves spaced out in front of them, My'ala, Aurelius and the four remaining builders passed a canteen of water between them, watching the final ebbs of the sun on the horizon with tired, blurry eyes. They were all sweat-stained and aching, their muscles worked to their limits – but with the knowledge that they had laid two innocent souls to rest, they hardly even noticed.

"Thank you all for your work this evening, my friends… you've done a fantastic job," My'ala proclaimed, lifting the canteen to the builders who all bowed their heads in return.

"You've honoured these people well with their graves," Aurelius said to her in reply. "I'm sure their spirits can now rest properly."

"I hope so too." She looked between the graves, and then up towards the sun. "We may well find out soon enough…"

"If I may ask… who exactly *are* these people that we've buried? You said you knew them…"

"It's a mother and her son, from a tragic story I was told by an old friend back in Arbash. As soon as you explained who the bones belonged to, I knew it had to be them…"

"I see." He paused, thinking. "And, from that, I suppose I should also ask: why did we make a third grave with nothing in it?"

My'ala felt her breath catch in her throat, as she looked across the piles of stones and saw the third empty grave at the far end. A well opened in her soul as she looked upon it: one that brought both tears to her eyes and a smile to her face.

"Because this mother and son had a father once upon a time, who I knew very well." She looked off to the horizon. "And, were he still with us, I know he'd want to be buried with them… so they could be together one last time."

Ahead of them, as the sun's golden orb slipped from view on the horizon, they looked on in awe as a burst of green light expanded across the sky, merging with the stars above like the waves of an emerald sea.

The builders at her side gasped and cheered; the God-Elect, nearly toppling over as he followed the ribbons of pearlescent light, was entirely speechless by the scene.

My'ala, meanwhile, simply sat in silence and smiled, looking up beyond the ribbons of light to the twinkling stars beyond. She saw constellations there that she remembered from her childhood. She saw shapes and colours and lights that scattered infinitely across the dark.

And at the centre of it all — so cosmically vast and incredible — she saw the two rounds of shimmering eyes studying her from above, with a thin mouth that curled up at the edges, so it almost looked like a smile.

Hello Artemis, My'ala thought, a glossy sheen over her eyes.

Welcome home.

—

ACKNOWLEDGEMENTS

This book is about journeys, and what we should look for in life to make us happy. It's a story of setbacks, and challenges, and self-reflection. It's a story that means a lot to me, and has been very cathartic to write, as its predecessor was and its sequel will most likely be.
So, I want to include here the few wonderful people who helped to make this book happen:

To Liam Fraser, my wonderful illustrator, who has been a true champion and overcome many of his own hurdles to bring this amazing cover to life, and to whom this particular book is dedicated;

To my ARC team, you wonderful bunch, who have supported me unequivocally on my writing journey so far;

And to you, the reader, for giving this plucky little book a go: it's a story that means a lot to me, and that I've poured a lot of my heart into creating, and I just hope you've enjoyed the ride – and maybe got something out of it yourself too!

So, with thanks, I wish you good tidings once again, and as always

Happy adventures!

HONOURS LIST

Giving a massive thanks to:

Jennifer Sutton
Ross MacBaisey
Henry Sinclair
Glenn Dove
Ganesh Subramanian Alwarappa
Jake Wilson
Joseph McLachlan
Sean Doty
Claudia May
Joanne & Nick Guy
Rebecca King
Chris Fisher
&
Esmay Rosalyne

For their support and contributions to the production and publication of this book and my future projects.
You are remarkable people, and have made a young man's dream come true.

I hope to do you proud.